# Eighteen & Desperate

*By J.W. McKenna*

**Other books by J.W. McKenna:**
Out of Control 1 & 2 (anthologies)
Office Slave & Office Slave II: El Exposed
Stripped & Abused
Controlled!
Sold Into Slavery
Boarding School Slave
Tied & Branded
The Politician's Wife
My Husband's Daddy
My Wife's Master
Torn Between Two Masters
Darkest Hour
Corruption of an Innocent Girl
The Sex Slave Protocols
Secretary's Punishment
The Abduction of Isobelle
Starlet's Fall
Joanna's Surrender
Slave to the Firm
She Couldn't Say No
Lara's Submission
Remedial Sybian Training
Trailer Park Tramp
Her Personal Assistant
Kyla's Basic Training
The Cheater
Training Bra
Two Girls in Trouble
Punish the Slaves
Landlord Ladies
Trained in Two Weeks

Copyright @ 2010 J.W. McKenna
All rights reserved.
ISBN: 978-1453746813

# Chapter One

Jerry Rissoli pushed his cart down the corridors of Westmont High School, his eyes roaming as if looking for wayward scraps of paper, but he was really checking out the cute girls. It was a harmless pastime and he knew better than to risk his job by flirting with a teenager.

"Hey, Mr. R," a hulking student called out to him and he smiled and nodded in return.

"Hey, Darren—I heard you guys beat Ashland yesterday. You got a homer, didn't you?"

"You bet! I drove in two runs in the ninth, iced the win."

"Great. Good job."

He liked being the friendly janitor and would often ask the kids how they were doing and express concern over their problems. Because he wasn't an important part of the school hierarchy, students seemed to accept him as a sympathetic ear.

He moved on, nodding and smiling and occasionally stopping to empty a trashcan or pick up some papers. It was a matter of pride to keep the school clean.

Many people would reject this lowly profession, but for Jerry, it was the perfect job. It wasn't difficult to do and it paid well enough. Plus, he had a decent benefits package. The fact that he was surrounded by giggling girls who would call him by name was an added bonus.

"Hey, Jerry!"

He turned to see Angela Ross, the head cheerleader. He smiled although he did not like her. She was a gorgeous blonde, tall and lithe, sought after by every boy in the school, but she had a poisonous personality. She liked to torment people, just for sport.

"Hi, Angela. You girls going to state this year?" Nearly every year, the cheerleading squad competed in the state championships.

"You bet, although Melissa's loss hurt us."

He frowned. He knew Melissa Younger, so full of energy and spunk. She had injured her ankle a week ago and was not expected to compete. "How's she taking it?"

"Oh, I don't know. She's upset about the ankle, sure, but there's something else bugging her, but she won't say what it is. I'm guessing she's still upset about her ex-boyfriend Tom. Hell, maybe she'll talk to you, huh?" Angela winked and gave him a salacious grin.

"I'm not sure what I could do."

"Maybe you could be her next boyfriend – I hear she likes the slackers."

His frown deepened. Tom, who had gone off to college last year, had already dropped out and joined the Army. To Angela, he was a total loser who had thrown away a scholarship. To compare him with Jerry the janitor was an insult to both men.

He shook his head and pushed his cart past the smirking girl. He wasn't angry because he knew how that girl would end up – without a friend in the world. She was only popular now because of the unique nature of high school: the insulated cliques with their strange pecking order that rewarded people like her. Once she was in the real world and she pulled that crap, she'd be ostracized within a very short time. Her world would come crashing down around her.

*Karma's a bitch, bitch*, he thought and smiled to himself.

Jerry kept his eye out for Melissa. He was worried about her. He knew a little bit of her story – she was an orphan, living in a group home over on Lancaster. Angela had tried to make sport of that fact and Melissa, small and shy as she was, nearly took the girl's head off. It was the last time Angela teased her about her situation.

He spotted her sitting by herself in the courtyard. She had her head down and was reading a book, but she hadn't turned a page while Jerry watched as he moved about picking up papers. His eye roamed down to her right ankle, encased in a soft walking cast. He'd heard it was fractured and she should make a full recovery – but only after the state championships. He pushed his cart close and began to empty a trash can nearby.

"Hi, Melissa, you look kinda down in the dumps today," he opened. If she didn't want to talk to him, he was prepared to leave quickly.

She looked up and gave a thin, brief smile. "Oh, hi, Mr. R." Melissa was only averagely cute, but she was still considered a knockout by the boys because of her gymnast's body, topped by generous breasts. They probably were only C-cups, but on her petite frame, they looked large. The rest of her body was perfect: narrow hips, flared waist, tight butt and muscular legs.

Unfortunately, her eyes were a bit too close together and her brown hair hung limply around her shoulders. Normally, she kept it tied in a ponytail, which helped, but today she had it loose about her face as if trying to hide from the world.

"Anything I can do to help? Maybe steal you an ice cream bar from the cafeteria?" He said it as a joke but she didn't smile.

"Naw, I'm all right."

"You don't seem all right." He cocked his head. "You want me to mind my own business?"

Melissa looked up at him. "No, you're sweet to care. This state sure doesn't."

"What do you mean?"

"I'm aging out of the system. Do you know what that means?"

"Not exactly."

"I've been at that group home since I was twelve and have really gotten to like the people there. We're like a big family, you know?"

Jerry nodded.

"Well, Nancy, the gal who runs the place, told me yesterday that I have to move out next month, when

I turn eighteen. It's called 'being emancipated' and it's supposed to be a big deal, like you graduated or something. You go before a judge and are declared an adult. But I don't have anywhere to go! I don't graduate for two months, so what am I supposed to do?"

"Don't they have programs for people like you?" Jerry couldn't imagine the state of California would just toss kids into the streets.

"That's what's fucked," she said. "They used to, but they all got cut because of the budget mess."

"You're kidding me... Can't that Nancy lady help you?"

"She said she's trying. She was nearly crying, telling me this. She said her hands are tied."

"So... what? You just move out and live under a bridge somewhere?"

"Yeah, that's about the size of it."

"I can't believe that. That's ... inhuman."

"You're telling me! It's like they want me to rush out and get a job and maybe skip the last month of school. I guess that's what I'll have to do. Maybe I have enough credits to graduate, I don't know." She shook her head.

Jerry made a sudden, insane decision, without giving it any thought. He found a scrap of paper and jotted down his address. "Look, this is crazy, what you're telling me. I'm sure they'll come up with something. But if they don't, before you go live on the streets, come by my place. I can put you up for a little while." He held out the paper.

He caught her wary look. "Oh no, it's not like that. I have a two-bedroom house – you'd get the guest room. It had a door that locks, okay? I'm not trying to make you feel uncomfortable. No hanky-panky. It would just be temporary, until you found a place or graduated. I'm not going to sit by and let one of Westmont's cheerleaders live on the streets like … well, like a homeless person!"

That brought a small smile to her lips. She took the paper. "Well, thanks. I hope it won't come to that. Uh, I mean… well, you know what I mean."

"I do. I realize it's what you'd call your last resort. But I don't want you living under a bridge."

"Yeah, it sucks. Well, thanks, Mr. R."

"You bet."

He took that as a cue to leave and he pushed his cart away, his mind spinning. Had he really just invited a sexy high school kid to live with him? It would be a huge risk to his reputation and maybe his job. On the other hand, he really couldn't believe the state would just force Melissa out like that. She would be vulnerable to every predator out there. He would much prefer to have that cute gymnast's body under his own roof. His cock swelled with the very thought. He dismissed it at once, knowing it would never happen. Surely her group home would find her a place.

\* \* \*

*Well, that was odd*, Melissa thought, watching him walk away. She'd never expected he'd ask her to live with him! Of course she knew what he wanted. Men were so transparent. He seemed harmless enough, but it was the quiet ones you had to watch out for, wasn't that what people said? When the serial killer was revealed next door, neighbors always said, "But he was so quiet! And he seemed so nice!"

No matter. She wouldn't be needing his help. Surely Nancy will come up with something! Might be best to avoid Jerry for the next couple of weeks. Just to be safe.

\* \* \*

Melissa was busy helping cheerleading coach Ms. Dixon rehearse the girls' routines for the next few weeks and Jerry only had a chance to smile and nod at her in the hallways. It must kill her to watch and not be allowed to participate, he thought, hobbling about on her cast as she was.

He wondered if she thought he was a creep for even offering his place. He didn't consider himself an ugly man – he had dark Italian features and a full head of hair. It really was his age that was the issue here. At thirty-seven, he was more than twice Melissa's age. No cute young girl wanted to hang around some middle-aged guy, even if he had promised no hanky-panky.

The team was headed to the state cheerleading competition in mid-May and everyone was sure Westmont would do well. Angela, as poisonous as she was, knew how to run a squad. And the cheerleading coach had been on a winning team when she had been in high school, so she had a few tricks up her sleeve.

Jerry was convinced that Ms. Dixon or one of the other girls' parents would offer to put Melissa up until she graduated. There was no way she would be allowed to go homeless. And certainly they'd all be appalled if they heard the horny janitor had offered to let her stay at his place! No doubt they would think he had ulterior motives.

And, actually, he did, not that he'd admit them to himself. He really just wanted to make sure she was all right, he told himself.

Sure.

# Chapter Two

When the knock came on his door the following Friday afternoon, Jerry expected to see a salesman or a Bible thumper and he frowned as he opened the door. He was shocked to see Melissa standing there, suitcase in hand, one leg still in her velcro boot, with tears running down her face.

"You're kidding me," he said. "They couldn't find you a place?"

She shook her head, unable to speak.

"What about the cheerleading squad? Or Ms. Dixon?"

Another shake of her head. She found her voice. "They're all at state right now. Maybe when they get back."

"You weren't invited to go with them?"

"Only active cheerleaders can go. Ms. Dixon said they couldn't afford to send me." More tears fell. "Happy fucking birthday, huh?"

"Well, come in! I'm sorry to keep you standing out there. I'm just stunned."

"You and me both. I thought something would happen, right up until I was told to pack my suitcase."

"And that's it? What about the other cheerleaders' parents?"

"They're all at state too. So I'm looking for something VERY temporary."

"Of course!" He was delighted, but he knew better than to make her feel uncomfortable. "Let me show you to your room."

He led the way down the hall to the spare bedroom. He only used it for visiting relatives, so it remained neat and clean, the double bed made. It was a small room and the bed and a dresser took up most of the space. He showed her the closet and told her to make herself at home.

"It's wonderful!"

"Oh, and one more thing," he told her, grabbing the door. He pressed the lock and it made a loud click. "See? The door locks. No hanky-panky!"

She laughed. "I trust you, Mr. R."

"I'm glad. I still can't believe no one could take you in. I'm frankly appalled at the system. It sucks."

"You're telling me! Nancy couldn't stop crying, the girls were terrified, thinking they'll be next unless they can fix things – it was all a fucking mess."

"Well, I was about to start dinner. So just get yourself situated, the bathroom's just down the hall, you can put whatever you need in there."

"Um, do you have a bathroom too? I mean, in your room?"

"No, this is a two-bedroom, one-bath home. We'll have to share. But don't worry — the bathroom door locks too!"

She laughed and Jerry recognized it as a laugh of relief. "It'll be fine. It's just until Monday, when the girls get back. I'm sure I'll find a place then."

"Of course. You can stay as long as you want. I'm happy to have some company."

He went out and started dinner, a big grin on his face. He realized he needed a few more ingredients, now that he had another mouth to feed. He called out, "I have to go to the store for a sec, be right back!"

"Okay."

\* \* \*

Melissa needed some time alone to think. This was the last place she expected to end up! That damned Nancy! She promised she'd find something, but everything fell through. And with all the cheerleaders away, she was stranded. When she remembered Jerry's offer, she almost didn't even mention it. Poor Nancy had been ready to cry when Melissa finally took pity on her and tossed it out, as a casual idea, hardly worth mentioning.

"I've tried everything, Mel, I'm so sorry," Nancy had said. "I'm not giving up. Legally, you can't stay here and I've got another girl slotted for your bed, but maybe I can let you sleep in the hallway until we figure things out, okay?"

The hallway did not appeal to her – girls stepping over her on the way to the bathroom? Ugh. "Um, well, I may have something. Kind of a last resort…"

"Really?" Nancy had sat up at once, very attentive.

"It's not something I was seriously considering… It's the janitor at my school. He says he has a spare room."

"Really? Uh. Is he someone you think you can trust?"

"I guess. He seems nice enough. Keeps to himself. He's nice to all the students."

"Boy, I don't know. Give me his name and let me run him, see if he has a criminal record."

Melissa had given it and Jerry had turned up clean. Not even a parking ticket. It made her feel a little better.

"Look," Nancy said, "I know this is unorthodox, but it's only until Monday, right? Then the cheerleaders come back and you can bunk with one of them."

"Yeah. I guess."

And it was all settled. Nancy helped her pack up and had her out the door and dropped off in front of Jerry's house before she could even think about what she was doing. Nancy didn't seem to care, as long as she was out of her hair. She hadn't even bothered to come up and meet Jerry! What if he turned out to be a rapist? Would she be safe here?

She hoped to God she would be. Otherwise, the state of California will have a lawsuit on its hands!

\* \* \*

Jerry drove down to the grocery store and picked some extra chicken and hamburger and tossed in a few favorite teen items, like pizzas and frozen treats. On the way out, he passed the bakery section and on the spur of the moment, added a small cake to the cart. It had caught his eye because the colorful frosting spelled out: Happy Birthday!

Melissa was still in her room, so Jerry was able to

sneak the cake into the kitchen. He hid it in an upper cabinet. He realized he had neglected to buy birthday candles, so he rummaged around in his junk drawer until he found the stub of a taper and shoved that down inside the center of the cake. He started on a quick dinner for two.

Melissa came out a half-hour later and marveled at the food he was setting out on the table. "Oh, that looks so good, Mr. R! Uh, I hope I'm not eating you out of house and home."

"Nonsense. I'm happy to have someone to cook for."

"I'm surprised you aren't married yet, a handsome guy like you."

He smiled. "That's nice to hear, but unfortunately, most women my age want something more in a guy than a janitor, I'm afraid."

"Oh, I can't believe that! They can't be that shallow."

He shrugged. "All I know is, whenever I meet a girl and I think things are going well, I can see the expression on their face change when I tell them I'm a janitor at a high school."

"Well, I think you're pretty neat."

Was she flirting with him? He dismissed it as simply as gratitude and told her to sit. They dove in without preamble. For a small girl, Melissa ate a lot. Jerry made a mental note to go get more food at the earliest opportunity – and just as quickly he realized she would be gone soon. He felt a pang of disappointment.

"Didn't they feed you at that group home?" he

teased.

She looked up, her mouth full. She swallowed. "Uh, sorry. I guess I'm not used to seeing so much food. At the home, the portions are strictly controlled. Whenever anyone asks for more, they are told…" her voice changed, " 'Of course, dear! Just ask who would like to do without first!'" She giggled.

"God, it must've been like something out of Charles Dickens over there."

"Naw, they were actually quite nice. They just didn't have a lot of money from the state, you know. They have had to cut a lot over the last few years. It wasn't always that way."

"I see. Well, as a taxpayer, I'm angry. I've a half a mind to call my state representative."

"Trust me, Nancy's been doing that for months, years even. It won't do any good. Not unless you can find an extra twenty billion for the state."

"But kids' lives are at stake! What if a girl like you – or a guy for that matter – would up injured or dead because of this policy? The state would be sued and rightfully so."

"Maybe that's what it will take. No one seems to care right now."

"Hey, maybe that could be your job – child advocate. I mean, once you graduate. You could lobby Sacramento for more money."

"There are plenty of child services people doing that already. But it's a nice idea."

They ate in silence, each lost in their thoughts. After dinner, Jerry told her to sit still and cleared the plates.

"But I want to help! I can't let you wait on me!"

"Tomorrow, you help. Tonight, I have something planned." He disappeared into the kitchen. Taking out the cake, he lit the candle and brought it out.

"Hap-py Birth-day to you…" he sang, looking over the stubby candle at her delighted expression. She endured his off-key rendition and clapped her hands together.

"Oh, Mr. R! This is so cool! Thank you!"

"I figured maybe you needed a celebration. It's not every day a girl turns eighteen."

"I'm so glad I told you about my situation that day at school! I never would have had this otherwise!"

"You didn't get a cake at the group home?"

She tipped her head. "I got a cupcake. Everybody sang. It was nice." Her voice was flat and Jerry knew it wasn't all that nice. Bittersweet, more like it. Like the last meal for the condemned woman.

"Well, blow out the candle and make a wish. Wait, the other way around, I mean!"

She laughed. "Okay." She closed her eyes and nodded to herself. She easily blew out the single candle.

"Great! Can you share your wish?"

"If I do, maybe it won't come true…" she said. "Oh, what the hell, I'll tell you. I wished you'd find yourself a nice girl to settle down with."

Jerry was touched. He felt tears come to his eyes. "You wished that… for me? What about what you want?"

"I'm fine, now. I'm good."

They ate cake and Jerry apologized for not having

ice cream.

"Don't worry, Mr. R., it's not really on my diet."

"Oh come on, you can't be on a diet!"

"Well, it was for state, but that's all gone now."

"Great. I'll get some ice cream tomorrow."

She grinned. "Don't get me all fat!"

"I'm sure I won't have the chance," he said. "I mean, since you'll be leaving so soon and all."

She caught his wistful tone. "Hey, it's okay. You saved my life this weekend. I don't know where I would've ended up."

"How did you get here anyway? I hope you didn't walk!"

"No. Nancy dropped me off. I told her you were a friend of a friend and that you'd put me up temporarily."

"I'm surprised she allowed that. I mean, with all the regulations they have to follow and all. She didn't even come in to check me out!"

"I was pretty convincing. Plus, she had no choice. Her only alternative was to push me out the door and wish me luck."

"God, I could just see that! You, hobbling down the street, suitcase in hand. It's criminal what they're doing to you young girls."

"Tell me about it." She shook her head. "I don't want to talk anymore about that. It gives me a headache. Let me help you with the dishes."

"No, no, you've been on that bad leg long enough. Besides, I have a dishwasher. You go sit down and rest and I'll dump these in there and we'll have some coffee, okay? You drink coffee?"

"Oh yeah. But I hate to not help."

"When do you get your cast off?"

"Not for another week. It doesn't hurt any more."

"That's good. Tell ya what – if you're still here after you get your cast off, then you can help with the dishes."

"Oh, I'm sure I'll be out of your hair by then."

He turned toward her and said, "You're not in the way. This is a delight for me. I mean that."

She smiled. "Really? It's nice to finally be wanted somewhere."

"Well, you're always welcome here."

She paused a beat. "People will talk, you know."

"Let them. Ask them if they'd rather you lived on the streets – or maybe they'd like to put you up. I hate busy-bodies like that, always looking for the worst in people."

"Yeah."

She went to sit down and Jerry cleaned up the kitchen. He made a pot of coffee and returned to the small living room with a cup for each of them. She took it gratefully.

"I didn't know what you wanted in it."

"Milk and sugar, if you have it."

"I do." He went to the kitchen and fetched them and placed them on the coffee table. Melissa poured a dollop of milk and one teaspoon of sugar and stirred. She took a sip.

"Ahhhh! Perfect."

They sat and drank their coffees. Jerry wasn't sure what to say next. He felt like he was split in two. Part of him wanted to protect her, the other part wanted to fuck her. He realized it was just his dick talking. And his dick was telling him she was eighteen now.

"So what do you think Westmont's chances are at state?"

"Pretty good, but I think they're missing me. My replacement wasn't as good at some of the tumbling runs." She shook her head. "I guess that sounds like I'm bragging…"

"No, no – I've seen you girls perform, back before you hurt yourself. I thought you were the star of the show."

"Oh, come on… But thanks."

"Who is replacing you?"

"Barbie. Barbie Hapgood. She's okay. She'll do fine."

"I wish we could watch them on TV. I can't believe you have to miss it all."

"Yeah, it sucks. But that's life. I'm learning how to be a realist pretty damn quickly now."

Melissa put down her empty cup and yawned. "I'm sorry, I'm not usually such a light-weight, but it's been a hectic day."

"Of course! You don't have to stay up for me. I'll just put these away and head for bed myself."

"Okay. It's weird, having my own room. You know I haven't had my own room since…. well, since never."

Jerry smiled. "I'm glad to give you that chance."

"Thanks." She got up and walked with a minimal limp down the hall. He watched her rear end sway back and forth, the taut muscles rippling under her jeans. He felt his cock harden and it seemed to ask:

How can we convince her to stay?

*We can't*, he answered himself. *She'll be gone by Monday, so forget it.*

After she left the bathroom, Jerry heard the bedroom door close, followed by the click of the lock. He nodded. She didn't entirely trust him yet and that was completely understandable. Or maybe she just liked the idea of finally having a room to herself with a door that locked.

He got up and brought the coffee cups out to the kitchen and put them away in the dishwasher. He set it to run in an hour and checked his watch. It was only nine. A bit early for bed but he didn't want to watch TV and disturb Melissa. He went to bed and read, but his mind wasn't on the book. His hand stole down under the covers and he caressed his hard cock. He pictured Melissa's lithe body under his, naked and willing. His hand began to move. Within minutes, he came all over his stomach.

He slept quite soundly that night.

The next morning, he was up and in the kitchen early, cooking up pancakes. It was Saturday, so he had the day off. He had been planning to work on the yard, but now he really only wanted to hang around with Melissa. Of course, he had an idea that she might not want that. He'd have to play it cool.

The pancakes cooled and Melissa still didn't show. Jerry cursed himself, realizing that teenagers can sleep until noon without any trouble at all. He went ahead and ate and cleaned up his dishes.

It was after ten when she finally got up. He heard

her head into the bathroom and took the plate of food and reheated it in the microwave. She came out, dressed in a ratty robe she must've had for years and smiled at him. His heart leapt.

"Any coffee left?" She looked a bit bedraggled, like she didn't sleep well.

"Yes." He grabbed a cup from the cupboard and handed it over. She nodded her thanks and poured some coffee.

"I made pancakes."

"Thanks." She added milk and sugar to her coffee and sat down. "Sorry I'm so… I don't know."

"Maybe you're just not a morning person."

"Yeah, that's it."

"Or maybe you're still kinda stunned by your circumstances."

"That too. I mean, I just can't believe the system they have here."

"Neither can I," he said, shaking his head. "It's criminal."

"Well, thanks again for rescuing me. You're really being sweet."

"You're welcome." He paused. "So, what are your plans today?"

She grimaced. "Go look for a job."

"Right before the end of school? What if they want you to start right away?"

Melissa shrugged. "I guess I might have to miss some classes. I doubt they'll flunk me now."

"No, probably not. But it seems a shame."

"Yeah, that pretty much describes my whole life."

"Oh, don't say that. Things are working out, don't

you see? You'll go from here to a nice home with one of the cheerleader's parents and from there you'll get a job, maybe go to college..."

"Ha." Her voice was flat, emotionless.

"You don't think you'll go to college?"

"Not unless I win the lottery."

"You can always borrow the money. They have programs for that."

"I guess."

"If you want to succeed, you really should have a college degree."

"Oh? And do you?"

"That's my point – I'm a good example of what not to do. Look at me, I'm thirty-seven, single, no prospects for advancement... Sometimes I wish I had gone to college."

"Yeah, but if you had, you wouldn't've been there for me when I needed help."

He smiled. "That's right. So maybe it all worked out okay."

"Yeah." She reached out a hand and touched his. "Thanks again, Mr. R."

"Call me Jerry."

"Okay."

Her hand stayed there for another long second before she pulled it away. "Well, you said you have pancakes? I should really get out and start looking."

"Coming right up." He put the warmed plate on the table and watched her dig in. She ate four before she pushed herself away from the plate and groaned.

"Oof. I'm full. Those were really good."

"Glad you liked them. Now, you go get cleaned

up while I do the dishes."

"You are a very neat person, Mr. R., and I mean that both ways."

He tipped his head. "Call me Jerry, remember?"

"Okay, Jerry."

When she came out of the bathroom, dressed for the day, she looked much better. Her hair was neatly combed and her makeup understated. She wore clean jeans and a pale blue blouse. Jerry could see the outline of her lacy bra underneath and he had to look away or risk an immediate erection.

"Well, what do you think?" she asked. "You think I look okay for job interviews?"

"Oh yeah." His voice sounded a bit strained. "You'll do great."

"Okay. Well, I'm off."

"Wait – how will you get around?" He knew she didn't have a car. "Do you need a ride?"

"Oh no, I'm a real pro with the buses around here. That was drilled into us from an early age at the group home."

"Oh. Well, do you have money for the fare?"

"Sure." She seemed so nonchalant, Jerry didn't push it.

"Okay. Good luck."

"Okay, see you later." And she was gone.

Jerry watched her head down the walk, her body taut and sexy and bit his lower lip. *God, what am I doing,* he asked himself. *This is just going to break my heart.*

It had been a long time since he'd last made love.

# Chapter Three

Melissa arrived home around four, looking worn out and sweaty. He didn't need to ask how it went, but he did anyway.

"How was it out there?"

"Brutal. No one's hiring. I mean, so far."

"Well, things might ease up as we get closer to summer."

She shrugged. "I hope so. Most of the managers I talked to seemed more concerned about the economy – they said sales are way down because of the recession and they can't afford to hire any new people."

"Somebody somewhere is going to need someone." It was a lame encouragement and Jerry regretted saying it at once.

"Yeah. I hope so. Otherwise, I *will* be living under a bridge."

"No, that won't happen."

Melissa looked up and caught his determined expression. She smiled. "Thanks."

"You look hot and sweaty. Go take a shower while I cook some dinner."

"I can help! At the home, we all took turns. If you didn't learn fast, you heard about it from the other girls."

He nodded. "Okay."

She disappeared down the hall and Jerry sat on the couch and mulled his good fortune. Too bad it had to end Monday, he thought.

\* \* \*

Huh, she thought as she headed into the bathroom. Jerry is turning out to be a really nice guy. He hadn't put any moves on her at all! Although it wasn't hard to see he'd like to, the way he looked at her with his puppy-dog eyes. That first night, she had expected him to try to jimmy the door and molest her in her sleep, but nothing happened. Now he was buying her food and making her dinner. God, a girl could get used to this.

Were there really men like this in the world? Had she misjudged him?

\* \* \*

Sunday afternoon, Melissa came home excited, her face bright, and Jerry was sure she had a job.

"You got a job?" He asked, ready to congratulate her.

"No, not that. I mean, I looked and all, but no, that's not what's so great." She paused, dramatically. "We took third in state!"

It took Jerry a moment to change gears. "Oh, state! The cheerleader championships! You heard?"

"Yes! I stopped by Angela's house, talked to her dad – I knew he was coming back early. He gave me the news." She tipped her head. "Maybe if I had been there, we might've gotten second or even first…" She looked up, her mouth ajar. "Oh! I guess that sounds like I'm bragging again."

"No, I'm sure they would've done better with the original team. It's always hard when you have to substitute at the last minute."

"Yeah, although Barbie had a good three weeks to practice with them. I'm sure she did fine. Anyway, they got a trophy and everything. It's pretty cool." She looked wistful, and Jerry knew it killed her not to participate.

He got up and touched her shoulder. "I'm sorry you couldn't be there."

"Yeah." Her good mood seemed to have evaporated. "Well, I'm going to shower." She went down the hall.

Jerry busied himself in the kitchen. When Melissa joined him, smelling fresh and clean, and offered to help cut up vegetables, he accepted at once, happy to have her nearby. "So, do you think Angela's parents might put you up?" he asked, just to fill the silence.

"Oh god no. I could never live with her. She's a bitch."

She was so frank, he had to laugh. "Yeah, I've noticed that too."

"I think Barbie's folks might be able to take me in. They have a spare room now that their son has gone to college."

"Great. That'd be great."

Jerry felt a sadness approaching and tried to make the best of it. The weekend had been a pleasant diversion from his dull life and he wasn't looking forward to being alone again. He resolved to try dating again.

The next morning Jerry had to jockey for the bathroom with Melissa, as she was trying to get ready for school. Finals week was coming up soon and she didn't want to miss a day. She had her suitcase packed and ready by the door.

They drank coffee standing up and each ate a piece of toast, covered with jam. It was almost domestic, the scene they were creating. Two busy people, trying to get out the door. Only one was going to work and the other was still a kid in school.

"Come on, I'll give you a ride."

"Oh, okay. Thanks. And I mean, for everything."

"Okay. And if the deal with Barbie doesn't work out, you've always got your last resort, okay?"

She grinned. "Okay, Jerry."

As he drove toward the school, he felt that sadness return. But it really was for the best. No way should he be fooling around with an eighteen-year-old! He should have his head examined. But that wasn't the part of his body that thought having a sexy teen-aged girl around was a good idea.

School was bustling and Jerry wondered if people noticed him pull up and park with Melissa in the car. In hindsight, he probably should've dropped her off a block or so away, but it was too late now. Let them talk. Let Melissa explain how she was forced out onto the street and that Jerry rescued her. She'd tell them he was a perfect gentleman. Not that they'd believe her. Or him. People wanted to think the worst of others.

"Bye," he said as she got out, dragging her suitcase. "You going to be okay with that thing?"

"Yeah, I'll dump it in Ms. Dixon's office for now. Thanks," she said, already distracted. She hurried off without so much as a backward glance.

He went in and found Frank Sawyer, the senior janitor, drinking coffee in the small storage room that they used as their office. Frank had been at the school for nearly fifteen years and was probably pushing forty-five. Tall and balding, he was an underachiever just like Jerry, but he had managed to find a good woman who would take him as he was. Jerry envied him.

"Hey, Jerry, how's it hanging?" Frank saluted him with the half-filled coffee cup.

"Good, real good. Looking forward to those summer hours."

"You and me both."

During the summer, they worked nine to four, shaving an hour off each end of the day. It wasn't much, but it made a huge difference in their attitudes. It was like taking a mini-vacation every day. And because they had both set up their paychecks to remain the same all year long, they didn't suffer any loss in income.

"Lot of projects this summer?" Jerry asked.

"Same old shit. Paint doors, change combinations. Nothing special that I've heard about."

"Huh." Jerry looked forward to handling a special project, just to break up the monotony. Painting doors was the worst part of summer. Every door had to be sanded and repainted to hide the scuff marks and dents. Considering there were two hundred doors in the school, the job became tedious rather quickly. "Oh boy."

"Yeah. Job security, right?"

"Yeah. Well, I guess I'll start making the rounds."

"Okay. I'll hold down the fort here for a while longer."

Because Frank had seniority, he got to do a lot more sitting around. Jerry grabbed the cart full of cleaning supplies, brooms, a mop and bucket and large trash can and pushed it out of the small space.

Jerry caught only glimpses of Melissa during the week. Each time, she'd smile and nod and he'd nod in return, but they didn't have a chance to talk. It was the week leading up to finals and she and every other student were busy cramming a year's worth of knowledge into their tiny, unformed brains. School seemed to fairly buzz with energy.

The weekend came and Jerry spent his days off puttering around his yard, planting some tomatoes and peppers in his garden and weeding the flowerbeds. His heart wasn't in it, but he told himself to snap out of it. He was better off not to be tempted by such a young girl.

Finals week – the last week of school – was notable by the sullen, deadened faces of the teenagers as they drudged their way from class to class, their hopes for good grades being crushed by the reality of the difficulty of the exams. Jerry saw Melissa with the same expression and wanted to tell her to cheer up, it would be over soon. But he didn't have a chance to stop her and talk.

The black mood broke on Wednesday for seniors,

who finished their last exams and were released from the bondage of high school. The underclassmen, who had to endure two more days of torture, watched them sullenly as they whooped and cheered and signed yearbooks. Because Melissa was a senior, she was done today as well, and Jerry made a special effort to run into her. He noted right away she was no longer wearing her boot. He caught up with her just as she had separated from a group of friends, her yearbook clutched to her chest.

"Hey, congratulations," he said. "For both things." He pointed at her right leg.

She smiled bright enough to blot out the sun. "Oh, hi, Jerry! Isn't it great! I got my cast off yesterday and now, yippee, no more school! Maybe forever."

She saw him blanch and laughed. "Oh, don't worry, I'll probably go to college. Thanks for all your help."

"You're welcome. And yes, I hope you do. You don't want to end up like me!" He'd said it as a joke but he also meant it.

"You seem pretty happy, you know. You've got a nice house, you have a job you like – what's so wrong with that?"

"I guess I just want more for you kids, that's all."

" 'You kids!' You make yourself sound so old! You're not that old."

"Somedays I feel old. Like today, for example. All you ki—uh, students, are going out into the world, fresh-faced and eager, and I'm stuck here."

"Oh, I think in this economy, half the students here would kill to have a good job like yours."

Jerry had to agree with her. They were heading out into a brutal job market. "Have you had any luck yet?"

"No, but I haven't been looking much. Had to study. But I'll be going out again tomorrow, full time."

"I wish you luck. I'm sure your personality will convince some manager to give you a chance."

"Thanks, that's sweet of you." She looked around. "Well, I gotta go. See you around, okay?"

"Okay – oh, wait!" She paused and he rushed on, "How's it working out at Barbie's?" He regretted the words as soon as he said them because it made him sound lonely and desperate.

"Oh, it's fine. Just fine." There was something in her voice he couldn't identify, a hesitation.

She waved and he watched her leave and realized it might be the last time he ever saw her. And his poor dick responded: *Now I'll never get to fuck her!*

"Oh shut up," he muttered.

\* \* \*

Melissa walked away quickly, wondering why her life always seemed so fucked up. When she had moved in with Jerry, she expected him to try and touch her and he never did. But when she moved into Barbie's house, her dad had started in almost the first day. Nothing outrageous, just a brief pat on a shoulder or back, but it made her feel creepy. She was so damned grateful to have a place, she didn't dare say anything. It was obvious what he was doing and he always made sure to do it when Barbie and her mom weren't looking.

He was overweight and bald and she did not want anything to do with him. But she owed him and he let her know it.

"So glad you're here," he had said just yesterday, trapping her in the hall while Barbie and her mom were in the kitchen. "I understand you were just about out on the street, huh?"

"Yes, Mr. Hapgood. The programs all got shut down for girls like me."

"That's a shame. But I'm happy to provide a place. You appreciate it, don't you?"

"Oh, yes, Mr. Hapgood."

"That's good," he'd said, putting his hand on her shoulder and giving her a little squeeze. "That's real good. I'm happy to have you here."

She had sidled by and escaped to the kitchen. She knew that wouldn't be the end of it.

\* \* \*

Both Frank and Jerry had to work hard to keep up with the mess the students made that week, cleaning out their lockers, throwing away papers and generally having a good time. There were the water gun fights, the pranks, the occasional spray painted slogans they had to deal with, but by Friday afternoon, they were satisfied they'd managed to keep the school in halfway decent shape. At least until they could return Monday and start again.

"You got any plans this weekend?" Frank asked him as they were putting away their carts.

"Nah. I'm going to sleep a lot and hang around the house. Try to gear up for the summer chores."

"Yeah, I hear ya. Let's just hope we don't have

some vandalism over the weekend to deal with."

Jerry nodded but his mind wasn't on the conversation. He was still thinking about Melissa. *Stupid old fool*, he told himself.

The weekend seemed to drag by. Jerry didn't go anywhere and tried to occupy himself with busy-work. He patched a hole in the garden hose, repainted the garage door and added a few vegetable plants to his garden. He found himself looking forward to Monday when the monotony of the chores would allow him to turn off his brain.

It seemed to work. Monday, Jerry volunteered to start painting doors while Frank tended to other matters. It was solitary, boring work and Jerry just let his mind drift away while he sanded and painted, one door at a time.

Frank joined him on Wednesday and they painted doors in tandem, working their way down the outside corridors of B Wing. The sun was hot and both Jerry and Frank were in their summer uniforms of blue shorts and short-sleeved shirts, with their names sewn into an oval on their chests.

By Friday, both Jerry and Frank agreed that next week, they'd tackle a few different chores and let the doors sit for a few days. Neither one could face another frickin' door. Jerry's muscles ached and he kept stretching his back to try to work the kinks out.

He took a shower and had a solitary meal, watched some TV until ten and went to bed, dreaming about doors, endless doors lined up for him to paint.

The doorbell woke him up and he was disoriented. Was that his imagination? It rang again and he glanced over at the clock. It was almost midnight! He sat up in bed, thinking this had to be some mistake, only to hear it again. Grumbling, he could only guess what it was – someone had vandalized the school and they needed him to clean it up. It was probably Frank on his doorstep – or the cops.

He pulled his robe around him and went to the door. When he opened it, he was not prepared to see Melissa standing there, tears streaming down her face, her suitcase at her feet. He heard the screech of tires and looked over her shoulder to see a car pull away quickly and speed down the street.

"What the hell…?"

"Can I come in?"

"Of course." He stepped aside and she picked up her suitcase and came in. She plopped it down in the foyer while he closed the door behind her.

"I'm sorry for waking you up."

"Don't worry about it. What's this all about? I thought you were all set at Barbie's."

"I thought so too – until Barbie's dad put the moves on me."

Jerry's mouth dropped open. "Ooooohhh…"

In his mind, his dick immediately piped up: *Aw, shit, he ruined it for me!*

"Yeah. It was awful. I had my own room, you remember, and I thought everything was cool. But he'd been kinda flirting with me, you know, behind his wife's back. I tried to ignore him or act like he was kidding, but I knew he wanted me. God! The pig. Then he shows up in my room tonight after everyone had gone to bed and tells me how much it's costing them to have me around and that he's fine with it – as long as I'm willing to give him a blow job whenever he wants it and not say a word to anyone. He told me: 'I know you group home girls are used to trading sex for stuff.'"

"Jesus."

"So naturally I scream and Barbie and her mom come running and dad denied everything, of course. And guess what?"

"They sided with dad."

"Right. Damn right. I couldn't believe it. Barbie's mom called me a troublemaker and asked me if that's what they taught me at the group home. Barbie told me flat out that her dad would never do such a thing and why would I lie like that. Her dad told them I had tried to blackmail him and when he didn't go along, I screamed. It was awful."

"So they kicked you out, just like that?"

"I couldn't stay there after that! I told them if that's how they felt about it, I would leave immediately and packed up. They started to get worried, thinking how it would look if I left in the middle of the night and I told them not to concern themselves, I had a place to go." She looked into his eyes. "I do have a place to go, don't I? You meant what you said about a last resort?"

Without thinking about it, he took her into his arms. He felt her breasts press against his chest and she began to sob. "Of course I did. Your room awaits. Welcome back."

After she settled down, he picked up her suitcase

and carried it to her room and placed it gently on the bed. "Try to get some sleep, we'll talk more in the morning."

He started to leave and she grabbed his arm.

"Jerry – this means a lot to me. You have no idea."

"I'm glad you're here. I missed you."

She smiled and it was radiant. He felt his cock swell and he hurried to leave before she noticed. Back in his own room, he tossed aside his robe and climbed under the covers. His hand found his hard cock and he imagined her in her room, stripping off her clothes, climbing naked under the covers… His hand began to rub his hard cock and he came within two minutes. He cleaned up and drifted quickly back to sleep.

# Chapter Four

Saturday morning, Jerry was up by eight, unable to sleep in. Part of him wondered if he had dreamt last night's visit and resisted the urge to peek into Melissa's room to make sure she was really there.

He made coffee and drank it outside on the porch, thinking about what might happen next. He knew what he wanted to happen – his hard cock sliding into her warm wetness. But that was just a fantasy. He struggled to anticipate the reality of his situation. Having an extra mouth to feed would be a strain on his finances, but he could accept that. He knew she would want to get a job as quickly as possible and start contributing, considering how independent she was. More likely, Melissa would find another place to live, where she would be with girls her own age and where people wouldn't be gossiping about her. He had to accept the fact that this situation was temporary. He was her last resort and she would be constantly looking to improve upon it.

Nancy at the group home would come up with something, he was sure. Or another cheerleader family, provided the father could behave himself.

He heard some rustling inside and went in to find

Melissa was up early as well.

"Hey, it's barely nine, I'm surprised to see you up."

"Yeah, I couldn't sleep. Too upset, I guess."

"Yeah, I can imagine."

"Not just that stuff with Barbie's dad – it's about my life, my miserable life." She caught his look. "Oh, I don't mean you. You've been great. Hell, if it wasn't for you, I'd be toast. No, I'm talking about how fucked up everything else is. Breaking my ankle and missing state, being tossed out of my group home, and then forced out of Barbie's place because of her creepy father. If it wasn't for bad luck, I wouldn't have any luck at all."

"Hey, you have pretty good luck, if you look at it differently." He wanted to hug her again, but he resisted.

"Yeah, you're right. I'm sorry. I don't mean to sound ungrateful. But I don't want to be a burden, either."

"You're not."

"Well, I can assure you, I'm going to get a job and start paying some rent. It's the least I can do."

He shrugged. "Sure."

"I'm going back on the job circuit right away."

"Okay. Whatever you need to do to make you feel comfortable. But first, let's have some breakfast, okay?"

She grinned. "Yeah!"

He made French toast and they sat across from each other at his small kitchen table and talked about the type of job she might seek. Melissa wanted to hit up every fast food joint in the neighborhood. Jerry suggested she check out Craigslist before she headed out to keep her from spinning her wheels.

"Yeah, that's a good idea," she said before devouring her third piece of French toast.

When they were done and Jerry got up to clean the dishes, Melissa jumped up and insisted he let her do it. He smiled. It was nice having someone around to help out.

She went off to shower and get ready and Jerry fired up his computer and began scrolling for possibilities. When she came out of her room forty minutes later, Jerry had already identified several places for her to go.

"You need a ride?"

"Oh, no, I'm not going to ask you to do that. I'm sure you've got better things to do. No, I'll just take the bus."

"Do you have money for the bus?"

"Sure." She seemed nervous and looked away.

"Melissa."

She looked up.

"How much do you have, if I may ask?"

"I have enough – I did some baby-sitting this year. I'll be fine."

Jerry wanted to help her out, but knew her pride wouldn't let her. Instead, he simply nodded. "Okay."

She left a short time later, her spirits high, excited about getting her first real job. Jerry didn't have the heart to temper her expectations. He knew what the job market out there was like. A girl with a high school diploma would have had a lot better luck a few years ago. Now, she would be competing for minimum-wage jobs against those with college degrees. Everyone was desperate to work.

Then again, her bubbly personality might win over some manager and she could get hired over other qualified candidates.

The day passed slowly for Jerry. He dug in the garden, washed his car and watered the back lawn. He knew he should paint the trim all around the house, which had become quite weathered, but he couldn't face another paint job, at least not until all those damn doors at school were done. He made a quick trip to the store to pick up some extra food for Melissa.

It was four-thirty before he spotted her coming down the sidewalk. He was on the porch, drinking a beer. He waved and she flashed him a thin smile. That told him she'd had no luck.

"How was it out there?"

"Awful," she said as she came up the walk. "No one is hiring. I mean, no one I talked to."

"What about those ads on Craigslist?"

"Some had already been filled and I'm on a long list for the others. I guess I'll have to get up earlier. Oh, I gave them your number – I hope that's all right."

"Of course it is! Later, you can get yourself a cell phone so you can have some privacy."

"Thanks."

"You want something to drink? I bought some cokes and stuff."

"Oh, great! Thanks. I'm parched."

He followed her in and told her to help herself to anything she wanted. She poured a glass of cola and they sat across the kitchen table.

"I'm sorry you're having so much trouble."

She nodded. "Yeah. One guy told me he had twenty-five people who had responded within a few minutes after placing that ad! I can't believe how bad it is."

"Yeah, this economy sucks."

"It would help if I had some training in something. But I'm good for nothing but crappy jobs."

"Don't sell yourself short." He had a thought. "Maybe you need a resume."

"Oh, yeah," she scoffed. "I could put down: 'High school graduate' and that's about it."

"Oh, no – I'm sure you have many talents, much more than most girls your age."

"Why do you say that?"

"Because you grew up more independently than those kids who had the easy life. I'll bet you have skills you learned at the group home that you're not even aware of."

"Yeah? You think?"

"Yeah. For example, how did you divide up the chores there?"

"We took turns." Her face brightened. "But that was up to us, how to divide things up. Nancy would only get involved if there was some big disagreement. She told us we had to learn to work things out for ourselves."

"Right. See? And you are an expert at riding the bus, too. That's another skill – being able to figure things out quickly. You think those pampered princesses at high school could do that?"

She laughed. "Probably not. Most of them were afraid of the people they might see on the bus."

"I can help you make up a resume that would include some of those skills, if you'd like."

"Really? That'd be great!"

They spent the next hour drafting Melissa's resume. In addition to the skills they had already identified, it turned out that Nancy had largely turned over the food budget to the kids and let them chose what to buy. It taught them to live on a budget and not overspend on snacks.

"This is great stuff," he told her as he finished it. "You'll really look good to managers now."

"Oh, I can't wait! Thank you so much!" She hugged him from the side and he felt her breasts pressing against his arm. It made his cock swell and he shifted uncomfortably in his chair.

"You're welcome. But I have an ulterior motive, you understand."

"Oh?" She released him and cocked her head.

"Yeah, I want you making money so you won't feel so useless. You'd be surprised at how much better you'll feel about yourself and your future if you have a few bucks in your pocket."

"Aw, that's sweet of you." She gave him a peck on the cheek, which only inflamed his ardor more. "But you're forgetting another thing: I'll be able to help pay my way around here. I can't have you feeding me and all that."

"Don't worry about it. You can help clean up, if

you are worried about being a burden. But I can assure you, you're not."

"Well, thanks, and I will. I'm now your housemaid, okay? It's the least I can do."

"Okay." He couldn't help but picture her in a frilly French maid's outfit, dusting the furniture. His cock threatened to break out of his pants. He hunched over to cover it. He busied himself printing out copies of her resume and made her gather them up from the printer, giving him a chance to slip into the bathroom to calm down. When he emerged, she jumped into his arms, the papers in one hand.

"These are great!" she squealed. "Even I am impressed!"

His cock swelled anew. He kept his hips back as he accepted her hug so she wouldn't feel his erection. She pulled back and said, "I can't wait until they get a load of this!" She disappeared into her room.

Jerry went out to make dinner. Melissa came out a few minutes later and offered to help. He put her to work cutting up vegetables, which she did with practiced efficiency. "Hey," he commented. "You should look for assistant chef jobs too."

"Really? Just because I can cut vegetables?"

"You never know what's going to set you apart from other candidates."

"Huh. Maybe you're right."

After dinner, they relaxed on the couch and watched TV, the picture of domestic tranquility. Jerry resisted the urge to put his arm around Melissa, telling himself that's probably just the kind of thing Barbie's dad had done. She yawned at ten and said she was tired and headed off for bed. Jerry sat up a while longer until she was finished in the bathroom, then he went to bed and dreamed about her body underneath his, her face thrust back in passion.

Sunday, she was up by nine, reading Craigslist ads and Jerry said she should take a break.
"But I need a job!"
"It's Sunday, take some time for yourself or you might get burned out on the whole job search thing," he told her. "Maybe we could go for a hike or something."
"Really?"
"Yeah – if your leg is up for it."
"Oh, it's fine. As long as I'm not jumping up and down on it."
"I know of a nice hike over in Wicker Woods that's only about a mile and a half. It would do us both good to get out."
"Sure!"
They packed some sandwiches and each took a bottle of water and drove over to the park. The hike was easy and pleasant and they sat on a high point and ate their lunch and admired the view. It took most of Jerry's will power not to lean over and kiss her.
Melissa's leg held up well and he promised they'd take other hikes in the days to come. "It's an easy thing to do and it's free," he said, grinning.
"Yeah, free is what I need right now."
She helped him make dinner. He complimented her on her cooking skills.

"It's not hard when you just follow a recipe," she said. "Barbie said—" She paused and shook her head, no doubt trying to rid herself of the bad memory. "Barbie told me she was a lousy cook and didn't want to learn! Can you believe that?"

"No, but that's just what I was talking about earlier. Barbie is just another pampered teen who will need years of coddling before she can be independent. As much as you hate your situation, you already have the skills to succeed."

"Thanks, Mr. R – I mean, Jerry. You always make me feel better about myself."

"Maybe I should hang out my shingle: Dr. Jerry, teen-aged shrink." He laughed. "No, wait, that makes me sound like a teenager!"

"I'll bet you were a good guy, even back then. So many boys aren't, you know. They'll lie and scheme to get into a girl's pants."

Jerry inwardly cringed. It was exactly what he wanted to do and now the idea seemed remote. He wasn't about to ruin things by being like every other man she'd met. "Well, uh, I wasn't perfect. I wanted to have sex too, you know."

"Did you lie and tell a girl whatever she wanted to hear and then dump her afterwards?"

"Uh, maybe a couple of times, if I'm being honest. I was immature, just like those boys at school. But as I've gotten older, I've learned to be upfront about things." He felt uncomfortable admitting this fact to her, but he didn't want to lie, not now.

"Well, thanks for the honesty. I appreciate it."

"You're welcome."

They ate and talked about her plan of attack for the next week. She would get up early, she told him, and do a Craigslist search and head out, trying to beat others to the punch.

"By showing up right away, it will show them I'm a hard worker," she said.

"That sounds good. That plus your resume and you'll land something soon, I'm sure." He snapped his fingers. "Oh, I need to give you a spare key so you can come and go as you please." He got up and found a spare in the junk drawer and handed it over. "The lock is a bit sticky, so you have to jiggle it around first."

"Thanks, Jerry, this is great. I mean, I can't get over how nice you're being."

*That's because I want to fuck you*, his cock spoke up loudly in his head.

"Aw, well, pshaw."

She leaned over suddenly and kissed his cheek and gave him a quick hug. "Thanks. As soon as I get a job, I'll start looking for a place to live. You don't have to support me for much longer."

"Like I said, I don't mind."

"But it is costing you extra, I know it."

He shrugged. "Sure, some. It's not a big deal."

"I just like being able to pay my own way."

"I understand that – and it's a good attitude to have. Miles more mature than those high school princesses."

She nodded, pleased with the compliment. "Okay, now you sit and I'll clear and wash the dishes." She jumped up and waved away his weak protestations.

This is how it should be, she thought. Two people giving each other mutual respect and support. In the group home, everyone was always jockeying for position, trying to get the larger slice of pie or the best bed or first dibs on the Goodwill castoffs. She had grown up learning to be independent, never relying on anyone.

And then someone came along like Jerry and made her realize some people are just what they appear to be: Helpful, friendly and honest. She had sorely misjudged him. Sure, he still looked at her longingly, but he didn't make her feel uncomfortable. Not like Barbie's dad!

Maybe I could just stay here, she thought. Forget trying to weasel her way into another cheerleader's house. Who knows how that dad might react? Maybe they're all alike, those men. Maybe they lust after their own daughters. She didn't need to give them any more temptation.

She wondered, if she just didn't say anything about moving out, would he ask her to leave? She doubted it. He seemed to genuinely like having her around. And she liked being here. He made her feel safe.

And safe was important right now.

## Chapter Five

Melissa went out every day that week, sometimes leaving before Jerry did and often not coming back until after he arrived home at four-fifteen. He could tell from her expression that she had had no luck and offered words of encouragement to try to prop up her sagging confidence.

She went out Saturday as well, even though he could tell she wanted an excuse not to face more rejection. He couldn't come up with a reason she should take the day off, so she left and didn't return until three-thirty. She looked absolutely beat.

"I know it's hard, especially in this economy, but if you keep after it, something will break, I know it," he told her.

"I know. It's just so hard! I've just about walked my feet off, talked to a hundred managers, left dozens of resumes, filled out applications – and I've got nothing to show for it."

"All you can do is keep after it. What's the alternative – be stuck here with me forever?"

He said it as a joke and she looked up at him and smiled. "I don't feel 'stuck' – I feel saved. And protected. Thanks."

"Aw well, hell." The more she appealed to his better half, the less likely he was going to get laid. Damnit.

She took the day off Sunday and they went on another hike, this one more than two miles, and ate a picnic lunch at the top of a hill. She told him it was days like this that made her forget all her troubles.

Monday, Jerry and Frank tackled the lockers, replacing broken locks and changing combinations so no one could access their old lockers. It was another mind-numbing task that had to be done, only slightly less onerous than the job of painting doors, which still was not finished. The days ran together and by Thursday, he was really looking forward to the weekend.

He came home at four-fifteen, as usual, and found Melissa sitting on the couch in a funk.

"No luck today?" he asked softly.

She shook her head. When he came closer, he spotted tears in her eyes. He sat down next to her and patted her shoulder.

"Hey, now, it's not so bad. You'll find something."

She shook her head harder. "I can't. I couldn't even go out today."

"Why not? Just fed up?"

"No, it's not that." She turned her face fully toward his. "I ran out of money."

"Ohhhh," he said, nodding.

"I only spent it on buses. I never had any lunch or anything. And now I can't even do that!" She fought back a sob.

"Hey, why didn't you say so? How much does it

cost to ride a bus each day?"

"Uh, about three-fifty or four dollars, depending."

"So about twenty bucks a week, right?"

She nodded and quickly added, "But I'm not asking for anything!"

"If you don't, how are you going to find a job and quote, 'get out of my hair', unquote." He grinned when he said it so she knew he was kidding.

She flashed him a small smile. "But I just can't! It goes against everything I've been taught! I'm supposed to be so independent and all – I can't ask you to fund my job search! I'm sure you can't afford to feed me and house me and give me money besides!"

"I could probably afford twenty bucks a week. We could call it a loan, if you'd like."

"No! I don't want to be owing you a bunch of money! What if I don't find a job for two-three months? I'd owe you a small fortune! No, I can't do it."

"Well, what else can you do?"

"I'd like to earn it, somehow."

Jerry spoke off the top of his head. "What, like trading for sexual favors or something?" As soon as the words left his lips, he wished he could take them back. He knew it was his dick talking again and how it got a hold of his mouth was beyond him. It just slipped out.

\* \* \*

In her mind, Melissa knew he was joking. Her knee-jerk reaction was to be offended, but it made a lot of sense. What else did she have to trade with? Mr. Hapgood's words echoed in her brain: *I know you group home girls are used to trading sex for stuff.*

That wasn't true, but she was used to being independent. She worked for what she got. And Jerry had been so nice! All this time, he'd never tried to grab her or kiss her or make her feel obligated. He just provided for her and what was she doing in return? Washing some dishes? Big fucking deal.

It wasn't like she hadn't given a guy a blow job before! Tom, her boyfriend last year, had gotten plenty! It was either that or fuck him and she didn't want to get pregnant. That would have ruined everything. Tom was so easy to please – as long as he came, he was happy. She had gotten quite good at it, if she did say so herself.

Would it really be so bad to give poor Jerry a BJ now and then? She doubted he'd gotten laid in years. It made a lot of sense.

As long as he didn't fall in love with her. Well, any *more* in love with her. If he could do that, it might make for a nice compromise.

\* \* \*

The expected angry eruption from Melissa never came. She just stared at him and slowly, very slowly, began to nod.

"That's it," she said.

"What?! I was joking!" He pretended the idea was ridiculous, but his cock was at full attention now.

"No, come on, Jerry – I've seen the way you look at me. You like me, you'd like to have sex with me. I'm not stupid. But you've been a real gentleman for weeks now. You've gone above and beyond and never asked for anything in exchange. Hell, the least I could do is give you a blow job now and then."

His mouth dropped open. His cock began to have renewed hope. "You're... you're not serious."

"Look, it's a straightforward business deal, okay?" she continued as if she was discussing washing his car or mowing his lawn for the money. "Let's say, two blow jobs a week in exchange for twenty dollars – does that sound fair?"

"Uh... uh..."

"You pick the days."

"I, uh, don't know. I mean, it's a very nice gesture and all, but it's kind of illegal and all. Not to mention that I never expected anything like this!"

"It's not illegal if it's just between you and me. We're not going to tell anyone."

"But I ... I'm not sure I can. I feel I'd be taking advantage of you."

"No, you wouldn't be. Look, I don't have much to trade with and you're a nice guy and I could do this for you and we'd both win."

"Do you, uh, even know what to do and all?"

Melissa rolled her eyes. "Are you kidding me? I had a boyfriend for nearly two years. What do you think girls do to keep their boyfriends happy?"

"Uh, I guess I thought you guys just had sex."

"I wasn't on the pill and Tom hated condoms. So we compromised – I'd give him blow jobs and he wouldn't try to fuck me unless we were sure I was safe."

"Jesus." It was a bit too much information.

"Look, I can't in good conscience take money I haven't earned. You're probably kinda horny, being here with me around all the time. What's the harm?"

*It does seem like a really good idea*, his cock piped up. "Well…"

"Okay, it's settled then." She pushed him back on the couch and began attacking his belt.

"Wait!"

She paused, staring at him. "What?"

"Uh… I don't know. It seems strange, that's all. A couple of weeks ago, you were a high school student. I felt protective of my students, you know? It's hard to get my mind around this."

She smiled. "That's sweet. Now I want to blow you even more than before. Hell, I'll do this first one for free." She unzipped him and reached in to caress his hard cock. "Ohhh, it's a nice one."

"God."

He watched, fascinated, as Melissa eased his cock out and went down on it. She certainly did know what she was doing. Her mouth felt hot and slippery around his cock. Within five minutes, he was ready to erupt.

"I'm… I'm gonna come!" he warned.

She didn't stop and he shuddered and came inside her mouth. She coughed and pulled back and the second blast struck her in the cheek. The third squirt landed halfway on the couch and the rug. Jerry was in heaven.

Melissa spat his seed into her hand and grabbed a handful of tissues with the other from the box on the coffee table. She wiped her hand and face and sat back, a big smile on her face. "How was that?"

"Great! Just great! But I worry that I nearly choked

you there."

"Nah. You just came a lot! Caught me a bit off guard. I'll do better next time."

"Better?"

She grinned. "I know guys love it when girls swallow. Sometimes I can do it, depending."

"Depending on what?"

"Volume and taste. I can adjust to the volume if a guy's come doesn't taste too bad. Fortunately, you taste just fine."

"You sound like you've done this a lot!"

She shrugged. "We orphan girls have to go the extra mile to be popular sometimes."

"You sound so nonchalant about it."

"I just have a different attitude, I guess. Part of my upbringing."

"I see. Well, that was amazing. Let me pay you for it."

Melissa held up a hand. "No, no – I promised the first one free. Hell, I should offer you more than that for what you've done for me. I'm very grateful. No, we'll start Monday, okay? I mean, for my bus money. Between now and then, anytime you want a BJ, you just ask."

Jerry's mouth moved but no words came out.

She laughed and pointed at him. "You look like a fish!"

He smiled and found his voice. "I'm going to take you up on that, as soon as I recover."

And he did. Later that evening, just before bed, Jerry was sitting on the couch, watching TV with Melissa when his felt his cock stirring. It had recovered remarkably well and wanted to feel her sweet mouth one more time.

He cleared his throat, not sure how to broach the subject. "Uh, Melissa?"

"Um hum?" Her eyes were still on the program.

"You said, uh, anytime, right?"

She turned to him and caught his expression. "Oh?" She smiled. "Right now?"

"Well, it's only because you said, you know."

Melissa pushed him back on the couch and unzipped his pants. "Okay, big boy. You've earned it." She enveloped him into her mouth and he sighed contentedly.

It took longer this time, probably because he hadn't had a chance to fully recharge. But Melissa was patient and tender and he couldn't resist her ministrations forever.

"I'm... I'm gonna come!" he warned her and cupped his right hand around the back of her head, wanting to thrust his hard cock down her throat and resisting the urge. He bellowed and came and, remarkably, she stayed attached to him, her throat working, swallowing his seed. A small bubble of it escaped the corner of her mouth and ran down her chin. He squirted twice more before she pulled away, a big grin on her face.

"Better?"

"Oh my god yes." He sank back on the couch, spent.

"I'll bet you'll sleep well tonight."

For a moment, Jerry wanted to ask her to sleep with him and instantly knew it would be the wrong thing to suggest. "Oh yeah, you got that right."

"Just do me a favor, okay? Don't eat any broccoli or asparagus for a while. Those veggies make a man's come taste bitter."

"God, you know way too much for a girl your age."

She smiled. "Now you're beginning to learn my dark secrets."

"Yeah? I'd like to learn more."

She tipped her head. "Maybe later. But right now, I'm going to bed. I'm suddenly tired."

Jerry imagined that she wanted to go to her room to masturbate and wished he could watch that. Or better yet, help her out. But he was truly spent and all he really wanted to do was go to bed.

"Yeah, me too. Thanks."

"Thank *you*," she insisted.

* * *

Melissa sat on her bed and tried to sort out her feelings. Part of her was happy to finally have contributed to the household. She'd felt like such a mooch and no one was hiring. It had been surprisingly easy to give the poor guy a simple BJ. Jerry was so grateful!

Men's cocks were all pretty much the same, she'd learned over the last few years. Not that she'd had had a lot of cocks! She wasn't a slut. Besides Tom, there had been Ben and, when she had been fifteen, her first boyfriend, Sam. All of them wanted to fuck her, of course. But she quickly learned that they would happily take a blow job instead, allowing her to keep her virginity a while longer, until Tom came along. She had finally given in after a year of dating, thinking he was The One. But then the bastard went away to college and broke up with her.

Another part of her wondered if she was doing the right thing. She didn't want to lead Jerry on. He was nice and all, but he was way too old for her. It was one thing to suck the cock of a boyfriend, but quite another to suck a man's cock because you felt grateful or you owed him. The way he looked at her, with those soft brown eyes, made her feel like she was just using him. But he wanted to be used. She hadn't asked to come live here. He had offered, right out of the blue. She never expected she'd have to take him up on his offer.

The whole thing sucked. She grinned when she thought that. "Yeah, everything sucks, including me!" she said in a soft whisper.

It was rather exciting – and naughty – to suck Jerry's cock just because he was a nice guy who had helped her. She remembered that manager of the Burger King she had applied to a few days ago. He had called her back into his office, looked her up and down and said, "I might have a position for you if you're willing to be cooperative."

She had known in an instant what he meant and was highly insulted. She said evenly, "If you want to hire me to work in your restaurant, fine. If you are looking for a girlfriend, forget it."

"I don't want a girlfriend," he had replied. "But I would like to have my dick sucked now and then. That's worth hiring you right there."

His casual proposition had shocked her. She had fled, offended. Now she realized she was doing pretty much the same for Jerry. Except he wanted a girlfriend. She was the one trying to keep it a business proposition. It made her think.

*** 

The next day was Friday and Jerry asked if she needed money for the bus. She made a face.

"Uh, if it's okay with you, I'd like to take a break. I'm so worn out on applying for places, I feel like I need to recharge. I'll get back to it Monday, I promise."

"That's fine. I completely understand. I think you've done a great job so far. You've earned a break." He grinned.

"Yeah, okay. I'll clean up around here today and make dinner tonight, okay?"

"Sounds good."

He went to work, whistling. Even the prospect of more doors to paint couldn't put him in a bad mood. Frank noticed right away.

"What's up with you? You get laid last night?"

"No," he said, skirting the truth. "It's just a beautiful day and I'm so glad I'm employed."

"You got that right. I've been talking to my brother-in-law – poor guy can't find anything! It sucks out there."

"I know. I ran into some students who said the same thing. I don't know what they're gonna do."

"Probably resort to cannibalism, knowing some of those kids."

Jerry laughed. "Yeah, right. Come on, let's get to D Wing. Lot of doors waiting for us."

He couldn't wait to get home. The day seemed

agonizingly slow to him and he found himself checking his watch often. Even Frank noticed it.

"You got a hot date or something?"

"Uh, no. I'm just kinda anxious for the weekend."

"You and me both, but I'm not checking the time every five minutes."

"I guess I have been overdoing it." It was not quite three and Jerry didn't know if he could stand to work another full hour and change. "Hey, how about I take off early today, huh? Would you mind?"

Frank thought about it. "Boy, you've got something up your sleeve. Tell you what – I'll let you go early if you can tell me what's got you so hot and bothered."

"Uh, well… I met a girl."

Frank slapped his thigh. "I knew it! Damn, man, I knew it had to be a skirt. Is she cute? Is she The One?"

"She's cute, sure, but I don't think she's the one. I mean, we're just hanging out right now."

"Where did you meet her?"

Jerry thought quickly. "At the mall. She was looking at a display window and I just started talking to her."

"Whoo-ee! Sometimes I wish I was single again."

That surprised him. "You? I thought you were happily married."

"Oh, I am, as best you can be. You see, men were not meant to remain faithful. It's our instinct to roam around. Not that I'd ever want to hurt Debbie, no. But if I could mess around and not get caught… well…" He winked.

"Okay, I've told you. So can I go early?"

"All right – but don't make a habit of it."

"I won't, I promise."

Jerry was elated to be allowed to slip away early. He had no doubt that Frank would take off himself once Jerry was out of sight, giving both men a well-deserved break from the monotony. He quickly cleaned up the paint supplies and was on his way home within ten minutes.

When he pulled into the driveway, his heart was pounding, like a kid who had just asked a girl out on a date for the first time. His cock was already half erect, anticipating Melissa's warm mouth on it.

He came inside to find Melissa on the couch, watching TV. He broke into a big smile. She looked up.

"You're home early, dear."

"Man home, man want blow job," he said in his best Tarzan.

"Aren't you even going to look over your nice clean place first?"

He tore his eyes away and looked around. The living room looked the same, maybe a little cleaner. "Uh huh."

"Silly, not in here. I just dusted and vacuumed. Go into the kitchen."

Momentarily thwarted, he peeked into the kitchen and whistled. The counters gleamed, the floor was freshly waxed. "Wow, it's spotless!" He felt her beside him and couldn't resist grabbing her in a big hug. It was just an excuse to feel her body. "Thanks!"

"Ew! You stink. You're all sweaty. Before you get your treat, you gotta take a shower."

He grinned. "Okay. Wanna join me?"

She shook her head. "Oh no! I know what will happen if I do!" She pushed him down the hall. "Go."

He went, feeling butterflies in his stomach. He stripped down in the bathroom and jumped into the tepid shower. It felt good to wash away the day's labors and heat. He stepped out and dried off, his cock at half mast. He didn't bother putting on a robe, he just boldly walked out naked and entered the living room. Melissa took one look at him, his cock pointing the way, and burst out laughing.

"I know what you want."

"Oh yeah. Maybe you shouldn't've made the offer, huh?"

"No, you've been so sweet, I can't deny you."

He sat on the couch next to her. His cock grew harder and thrust straight up.

"I'm not sure I can get my tiny mouth around such a big cock," she teased.

"Oh? Biggest one you've seen, huh?"

"Well, *one* of the biggest…"

"You're killing me here." He pulled her close and felt her warm breath on his stomach as she stared at his cock. "Get busy, girl, or I might have to throw you out."

Her expression changed and he suddenly felt bad. "Hey, I was only kidding."

"I know you were, Jerry. But please don't kid about stuff like that."

"I'm sorry. I won't do it again. I like having you here, remember? I've told you that a lot, haven't I?"

"Yeah, I'm just sensitive to not being wanted, you

know? First the group home, then Barbie's place. I guess I don't have a sense of humor about it."

"It will never happen again. I really want you here and you can stay as long as you want."

She nodded. "Thanks." She caressed his cock. "Now, I guess I'd better get busy, huh?"

"Oh, yeah…"

The next few minutes were heaven to Jerry as Melissa made love to his cock with her mouth. By now she knew what excited him and she had him ready to blow within minutes.

"Wait, wait," he begged and she pulled back.

"What?"

"Can we… instead?"

She shook her head. "I'm not on the pill."

"Maybe I have a condom somewhere."

"No. Not yet. I'm not ready for that, okay?"

He nodded. "Okay."

She returned to her task and brought him to the brink again. Jerry pretended it wasn't her mouth that enveloped him, but her pussy and came hard inside her. She swallowed it all and pulled away with a satisfied expression on her face.

"God! That was so good!"

"You're welcome."

"And the house cleaning too. You're great to have around."

"Thanks. I'll start dinner soon. So tell me, why did you come home early?"

He hugged her. "I couldn't wait to see you again."

"That's just your dick talking."

"Well, it has been pretty vocal these last few days,

sure. But I really missed you. And not just because you give great BJs."

"That's nice." She got up. "Now, you need to get dressed. Can't have you sitting around on the furniture naked."

He smiled. "Why not? It's my furniture."

"Yeah, but it's just kinda ookie."

"Hey, I just showered!"

"I know. But go put on some clothes anyway, okay?"

He nodded and got up and padded down the hall. He found his discarded clothes in the bathroom and took them to the back room off the kitchen, passing Melissa who was peering into the refrigerator.

"Hey!" she said when she spotted him, still naked.

"I'm just dumping my laundry, don't worry." But when he returned, he grabbed her in a bearhug and pressed her breasts against his chest.

"You're a very bad man," she said.

"I know." He tried to kiss her and she turned her head. He kissed her cheek instead. He quickly got the message and let her go. "Hey, I'm sorry – I figured if you're sucking my cock, maybe you'd want to kiss me too."

"It's not like that, Jerry, and you know it. This isn't a romance. This is more of a business arrangement."

The words stung him.

"You don't feel anything toward me?"

"Gratitude. I feel enormous gratitude."

"But I'm not your type, otherwise? Why, because I'm a janitor?"

"Don't sell yourself short. It has nothing to do

with that. You're a sweet guy and my rescuer. It's just the age thing, that's all."

"Oh." He felt suddenly foolish, standing naked in the kitchen with this teenager. He stepped around her and headed for his bedroom. She didn't call after him to say she was kidding or apologize for the hurt. He realized she was just trying to be honest and not lead him on. He shouldn't feel unwanted.

But he couldn't stop the pain of her rejection.

He dressed in clean shorts and a T-shirt and returned to the kitchen. Melissa was standing over the frying pan, cooking up chicken breasts. She turned toward him and said, "I'm sorry, Jerry, I'm just trying to keep everything together, you know?"

"I know. You're right, I guess I am too old for you. It's too bad, but there it is."

"If I was ten years older…"

"I know. It's okay."

It was an impossible situation, he realized. Having her around, giving him blow jobs all the time, how could he not fall for her? And yet, he knew it wasn't love, not in the traditional sense. She had seen that clearly. They had been thrown together by circumstance and she was trying to make the best of it. The sex only complicated things. No wonder she didn't want to fuck him. That would only make things worse.

The silence lengthened between them. Jerry didn't know what else he could say. He felt conflicting emotions: anger, disappointment, sadness, lust and arousal. He pulled a beer from the fridge and opened it. He stared at Melissa's back as she cooked.

She seemed to sense it and finally turned to see him leaning up against the counter, watching her. "Maybe we need to discuss the ground rules, huh?"

"Ground rules?"

"Yeah. How we might live together until I can find another place."

"Okay."

"There's no romance, just business. It's ten bucks per BJ and you get two a week – you pick the days."

She was being clinical about it and Jerry could see the toughness her group home had instilled in her.

"Okay."

"And this is only until I get my first paycheck. Then I'll start paying rent – just until I can afford my own place. Maybe one of my girlfriends will want to get a place with me."

"Okay."

She crossed her arms under her breasts, the spatula still in one hand. "Look, Jerry, let's not make this any more awkward than it is, okay?"

She was being so logical and he was being a baby, he decided. "You're right. I'm sorry. I guess I thought maybe something was happening between us. Now I know it was just sex."

"Right. I'm sorry, but I don't want any misunderstandings."

"You're right," he repeated, hating it that this little girl was being more mature than he was. "I'm sorry."

"Don't be. It's only natural. I know it must be difficult for you."

"So I guess I can't fuck you for a few extra bucks?" He wished he'd been more circumspect. But it was a question he had wanted to ask.

"Not right now, no."

That gave him a sliver of hope. What did she mean, 'not right now' – did that mean that maybe later, she might give in? Or was she just anticipating becoming a prostitute? Because that's what was happening here: She was prostituting herself for a place to live and bus money. It was sad in many ways. She was forcing herself to pretend to like him – and blow him – for her safety and security.

He wondered just how far she might have to go before she found some other type of employment.

\* \* \*

Melissa concentrated on her cooking and was glad when Jerry finally left her alone to go watch some TV. She hadn't wanted to be so hard on the guy, but he had to be set straight. She didn't need a boyfriend, just a friend. Although her feelings were all mixed up because of the sex. And yes, BJs were sex, whether she liked to admit it or not. She did get turned on when she made him come, how could she not? Part of her wanted to fuck him, but that would only make things worse.

She hated this ying and yang of her thoughts. Life would be so much easier if she could just stick to one thing and not waver.

Would it really be so bad if she fucked him as long as she told him she wasn't in love with him? God, he was so grateful for the blow jobs, he'd probably buy her a car if she fucked him! Not that she'd do that. She might trade it for being allowed to live here a while longer. She did like being Jerry's roommate. After her disaster with Barbie's place, she didn't want to try and hit up another cheerleader's family. What if the same thing happened again? She was pretty much on her own here and if she paid her room and board with a BJ or even a fuck, what was the harm?

It really depended on Jerry, she realized. He can't fall for her. She would be gone soon. If she could ever find work. Fucking economy.

Another thought struck her. It was crazy, stupid. And yet, it wouldn't go away. It made a strange kind of sense. But she'd have to think about it for a while, sort out her feelings.

## Chapter Six

Once Jerry got over his hurt, he found a kind of rhythm to his life with his live-in maid and BJ girl. On Mondays and Thursdays, he'd get a blow job in exchange for twenty bucks a week. He usually paid her all of it Monday morning so she'd have money for her job search, but he preferred to wait until he came home so he wouldn't be rushed. He'd take a shower to wash away the sweat of the day and slip on his robe before heading out to the couch where Melissa waited to give him his much-needed release.

The weeks of July began to run out and she still hadn't found a job, despite her fancy resume. Companies just didn't seem to be hiring. She was becoming discouraged. Jerry took advantage of the situation by asking her that she remove her top before giving him a blow job because it helped stimulate him to see her naked breasts. He knew it was only a matter of time before she would be naked for him and how long after that before she'd agree to fuck him?

By the first week of August, Melissa's despair deepened. And her guilt.

"I can't keep doing this to you," she said one Wednesday after yet another day of fruitless searching. He had just come home and was still standing in the living room. Melissa had stood as soon as he had entered and clearly had been waiting for him.

"To me? What do you mean? I'm happy." He was as happy as could be expected, under the circumstances. What man wouldn't want a live-in blow-job girl?

"No, you're not. And I'm not. And I'll tell you why." She ticked her points on her slender fingers. "One, I'm not paying any rent or paying for food and I know it's a strain on you. I'm sure you didn't expect I'd still be here almost two months later. Two, I know you're kind of moping around, wishing I would change my mind about 'us.' And three, my being here is interfering with your chance to find a nice girl. Someone who isn't a mooch."

Jerry found her to be quite insightful, a trait he had come to admire.

"Okay, those are legitimate points, except maybe the last one, for reasons I've already explained. But what else can we do? I'm not going to toss you out."

"I've been thinking about that. First, I need to know how much it's costing you to keep me here."

"Uh, I don't know…"

"Come on, be honest. I know your costs have increased."

Jerry decided to tell her. It had been on his mind ever since she had rejected his advances. "Okay. Well, the mortgage is about a thousand a month…" He saw her blanch and added quickly, "But I'd be paying that whether you were here or not. Now, I'd say utilities have gone up a little bit, from the extra water and electricity and all. I'd say maybe twenty-five bucks." He paused, knowing that it was the food budget that would really shock her. "Now, food, that's another story."

"Have I been eating too much?"

He chuckled. "No, not really. There are two of us eating, that's all. Overall, food and utilities, having you here is probably costing an extra two hundred total per month."

"Okay, that's good. So I need to come up with two hundred in order to feel I'm not a drag on your finances, right?"

"Yeah, but how are you going to do that, Mel? I mean, without a job?"

"It's simple. You bring some guys home that I can blow."

The idea stunned him. He staggered back and found the couch and sat down. "I can't do that," he said, but immediately he thought of Frank.

"Why not?"

"Well, I don't think I know of anyone who might want a blow job, first of all," he lied. "Second, that's making my place a house of prostitution and I don't think the neighbors will like it."

"I'm not talking about a horde of men. Just a handful – enough to pay you rent."

"Like how many are you thinking?"

"Say, ten a month? Charge them twenty bucks for a BJ."

"And you'd just hand that money over to me?" He'd never imagined himself as a pimp before. The idea both excited and repelled him.

"I owe you that much. If there was more, we could split it."

"Jeez. Maybe I should get a purple Cadillac and a feather boa too."

"I'm being serious. It's the only thing I can think of to do. No one wants to hire me."

"It's not just you – it's this economy."

"That doesn't help, does it?"

"No, I guess it doesn't." He thought about her proposal. "But what about the bus money? You'd want to keep that the same?"

"I'd have to, wouldn't I? I still need to go look for work."

"Sure, sure." He was thinking: *If she was willing to fuck men as well as blow them, she wouldn't need to look for work.* He decided to take the chance. "I've got a proposal for you. It fits in with what you're suggesting."

"Okay." She crossed her arms under her breasts, a sure sign she was wary.

"I'll pay you thirty bucks right now, cash, if you'll take me into your room right now and fuck me. I'll wear a condom, of course."

She seemed rocked by that. "You'll pay me to fuck me?"

"That's what you're talking about doing here, isn't it? You think the men I bring home will be satisfied with just blow jobs? Maybe at first, sure, but over time, they're going to want more. It would be better to start with me."

"I don't think I want... I mean..." She trailed off.

He waited until she could organize her thoughts.

Finally she said, "Thirty bucks? That seems kinda low."

"Consider it the landlord discount. I'm sure when you start your business, you can charge a hundred bucks and men will pay it."

"You think so?" He could see the wheels spinning in her head.

"Sure. You're like every man's fantasy – a sexy, athletic teen-aged girl who will make them feel young again. You could charge fifty bucks a blow job and one hundred a fuck and get it. Maybe more."

"I'm not prepared to go that far. Not yet."

"And why not? You know how hard it is out there – and if you found a job, it'd be minimum wage, which is what? Eight bucks an hour? You'd be lucky to clear two-fifty a week, probably less because most employers only let you work about thirty-five hours a week."

"Really? Why?"

"Because then they don't have to pay for health care. So you might only make eight hundred a month. You know how much apartments around here cost? A one-bedroom goes for about nine hundred. A two-bedroom, twelve-fifty. Plus utilities. Even with a roommate, you're looking at maybe nine hundred a month just to live. You'll always be chasing after the next job or trying to land a second job just to pay the bills."

He paused and let that sink in. "My point is, you need to understand what you are getting into here. Yes, it will pay better than a regular job, no doubt. You could easily clear a couple hundred a day, maybe more. But it will come at a cost – and I'm not sure you're willing to pay it. This is not something you can ease into."

"You don't think so?"

"No. If you're going to do it, you have to understand that you'll be a prostitute. Saying you'll only give blow jobs is nonsense. What will you do if a john decides to force the issue?"

"That'd be rape!"

Jerry scoffed. "You actually plan to go to the cops and say, 'I only wanted to blow him for fifty bucks but he insisted on fucking me'? They'll laugh – before they arrest you."

"I never saw myself as a whore."

"Well, that's what we're talking about here. If you're not ready to fuck me for money, you're certainly not ready to take on other men."

She went silent and Jerry got up and went into the bathroom to shower. The girl was a puzzle. One on hand, she seemed so much more mature than other girls her age, but she could also be quite ignorant about the way the world worked.

What? Did she expect to blow a few guys and that would be it? Pay for her room and board? It was nonsense. Another part of him was glad she was having second thoughts. He wasn't sure he was ready to share her, even if she didn't want to be his girlfriend. In the back of his mind, he thought she might come around to love him. Hell, stranger things can happen. He was only nineteen years older – was that so awful? Did she look at him like an old man at thirty-seven?

* * *

Melissa sat on the couch and ran over her internal debate one more time. Jerry was right, she realized. If she decided to go down this road, men won't be satisfied with blow jobs. She wasn't a virgin, so that argument immediately fell by the wayside. So what was it? Was she being a baby? No, she was standing her ground, not giving into pressure to make money. Which meant she'd continue to be a mooch. Her head hurt.

Dammit, she wished she could just *know* what was the right thing to do!

One argument went like this: *It's not like you haven't fucked before! You fucked Tom like there was no tomorrow on those days when you were pretty sure you couldn't get pregnant! So what's the harm? Look at poor Jerry, he's just about got his tongue out on the floor! You need to pay your own way!*

The other argument came right back at her: *Blow jobs are one thing, fucking is quite another! Do you really want to become a whore? Sure, the money's good, but what about your soul?*

\* \* \*

When he came out of the bathroom, wearing his robe and carrying his dirty clothes, he was startled to find Melissa in the hallway. Her jaw was set.

"Okay," she said.

"Okay? Okay what?"

"I'll fuck you for thirty bucks, cash. Right now."

He stared at her. "You really want to do this?"

"Yes. You're right – it does suck out there. I've been looking for two months and I'm about all used up, emotionally. A girl can only stand so much rejection. You want me. You know what that does to a girl's ego? To have men want her, even if it's just for a quick fuck or a BJ?" She waved away his sputtering response. "No, I know what I'm getting into. I could be arrested. But you know what? If that happened, I'd tell my story – that I was forced into prostitution because the state of California wouldn't help me. Maybe that will finally shake things up for the other girls in the system."

"Wow." Jerry was impressed by her logic. "That actually might do it. Not that I'd recommend getting arrested."

"I was hoping that's where you would come in. You could watch over me, protect me."

"Be your pimp."

She shrugged. "If you could stand it."

"I could lose my cushy job. It's a huge risk." He shook his head. "I don't think it's worth it."

"But you were telling me how much I could make just a few minutes ago!"

"I know, but that was to shake you up and make you realize what you were really suggesting. I didn't think you'd thought it through. Sure, the money can be good – until you get arrested and have to pay a lawyer."

"Maybe we could start out small – just one guy or two that you know. Guys you trust."

"You'd really want to do that?"

"Yes. I'm not thrilled about it, of course. I figure it's just temporary." She paused. "It would help if I could get on the pill, just in case."

"Jesus." He found himself thinking about it. Could

he really keep it so quiet that the cops would never find out? The school district would fire him immediately if they found out and he didn't want to lose his job.

"Well?"

"I'm thinking, I'm thinking!"

"I don't mean about that – we can talk about that later. I'm talking about fucking me, right now. I know you want to."

He grinned. "Oh, that! For thirty bucks? Sure." He reached out and took her hand and pulled her down the hall to his room. He had been waiting for months to do this, ever since he had first talked to her at school.

Melissa was rightfully nervous so he took his time. He wouldn't let her strip – he slowly removed every piece of clothing himself, admiring the young skin that emerged and taking time to kiss it, first a shoulder, then a collarbone, then a breast – and another breast – until she was swooning as she stood there, her arms fluttering over his.

"God," she breathed. "I didn't know it could be like this."

"This is the difference between those young boys you've been dating and men," he told her. "Men know how to make a girl feel special."

"Yeah," she said, her voice tiny.

When her body lay bare, Jerry eased her down onto the bed and began to strip. She watched him. "Can I help?"

"No, you just lie there and look pretty."

He quickly removed his clothes and tossed them

aside. He lay down next to her and began to make love to her body with his lips and hands. She shivered and giggled and swooned. Glancing down, he could see the wetness shining through the brown thatch of hair between her legs. Easing down, he inhaled the fresh scent of a young girl's body and his tongue came out to touch the nectar there. She gasped and drew her thighs up. He pressed his hands down and pushed her legs apart, exposing her pussy fully to his gaze for the first time. It was beautiful. He touched the tip of his tongue to her clit and she made a small noise in her throat.

"God, Jerry, you're ... you're so good!"

"We've just gotten started, honey."

He licked and teased her pussy until her clit was standing up at attention and he knew from the noise she was making, she was close. He debated fucking her right now or letting her come first. He decided to be a gentleman. He licked her juices with the flat of his tongue and pressed his thumb against her engorged clit. She gasped, raised her hips and shook, making keening noises in her throat. It was a very good climax, he could tell.

"Oh god! Oh my god!" she gasped.

"I'm glad you liked it." He looked in the nightstand for a condom and found only an empty box. "Shit!"

"What?"

"I'm out of condoms. I guess it's been a while..." How could he have been so stupid? Would it have killed him to plan ahead, even it if didn't seem likely?

"That's okay – you can do it ... if you're careful.

You'll have to pull out."

"Sure!" He would agree to just about anything at that point. He slipped his rock-hard cock into her and she breathed slowly as it went in. She was tight, very tight. It was evident that she hadn't had much sex in her young life.

"You okay?" he asked solicitously.

"Yeah. Just go slow. Oof."

He eased himself deeper into her and marveled at how big she made him feel. He had always considered himself of average size up until that moment. Now he felt like a porn star. When he was halfway in, he began to slowly stroke back and forth to make his passage easier. Her eyes went wide.

"God, you're so big!"

He smiled. "That's right baby, I'm big, all right."

Her pussy was adjusting to his size and he found he could press in further. He didn't want to hurt her so he took his time, making sure she was getting as much pleasure out of it as she was. As he looked down upon her naked body, his cock almost all the way inside, Jerry couldn't believe his luck. He was fucking this cute, sexy girl! The girl he thought he had no chance with. His desire increased and he didn't want to come yet. He tried to think about something else.

He wanted a picture of this moment and wondered how he might accomplish that. Thinking about the logistics of it helped retard his climax and he tried to concentrate more on her pleasure. She was clearly into it – her head was thrown back and her hands clutched at his arms, as if trying to pull him all the way inside her. She made gasping noises and her body began to shudder. God! It made him so hot he couldn't stand it any longer and he felt himself about to blow.

"Yes!" She cried out, "Yes! Yes! Yes!"

That drove him over the edge and he realized he was just about to come inside her. He yanked back and sprayed his seed all over her pussy and stomach.

"No!" She cried. "No! I was so close!"

"I'm sorry – I didn't want to come inside."

"Oh, okay. That's good, that's good. I'm sorry."

"No, it's understandable. I wish I had condoms. I promise I'll go out and buy some right away."

"Okay. That'd be good. God! I was so close!"

"Well, I owe you one."

She looked up at him. "Oh? You trying for a freebie?"

That brought him back to earth. "Oh, uh, no. That reminds me." He got up and found his pants. He pulled out a twenty and a ten and handed it to her. Her expression was hard to read – caught somewhere between embarrassment and gratitude.

"Uh, thanks. Look, I didn't mean…"

"I know what you meant and you're right. This is business. I can't think of it any other way."

She didn't respond and he felt let down. Sure, he had come and that was great, but she didn't love him and probably never would. He'd never have a cute girlfriend like Melissa. He might as well troll the bars for some middle-aged ladies who weren't too picky.

He slipped on his clothes and went out and grabbed a beer. He was standing in the kitchen, thinking, when Melissa came out, dressed once again.

"I'm sorry," she said. "If this is going to be too hard for you, I can probably find another place."

"Like where? With one of your cheerleading friends? Maybe Barbie would take you back, if you agreed to fuck her dad." He didn't mean to sound so harsh but she had caught him before he could get his emotions under control. He realized from her expression he was about to sabotage a good thing. "Hey, I didn't mean that. I'm sorry."

"You're angry."

"Maybe a little. I'll get over it. I'm supposed to be the mature one, you know."

She gave him a brief smile. "I know. I don't like this either. I wish I could just earn a decent living. I hate being so dependent. That's not how I was raised."

"I know. But you aren't ready to live on your own. That's what's so fucked. You need me and I need you. Especially now."

"Because I let you fuck me?"

"Well, yeah. Duh."

"Just don't fall in love with me."

"I'll try not to." He grinned, although it was a false grin. "And don't you fall in love with me, either, young lady."

She smiled. "I'll try not to. Although after that ... session, it might be harder than I thought. Wow."

"And you didn't even get to come again! Just you wait."

Her smile broadened. "Yeah. I can't."

Reality struck when he realized it would cost him.

"I'm not sure I can afford it, though."

"Oh, about that." She reached into her pocket and pulled out the cash. "Here, put this toward my food bill or something." She placed the money in his hand.

"So what was that all about in there? Why the charade?"

"I was trying not to let our emotions get in the way, silly. It seemed to do the trick."

He nodded slowly. "Yeah, it did."

She was pretty damn smart, that kid.

# Chapter Seven

Melissa sat in her room, wrapped in her robe, fresh from a shower. She felt tingly all over, like she had just touched an electrical wire. Jerry had proved to be a surprisingly good lover. That she had not expected. She had thought she'd just "do her duty" and not get emotionally involved.

*Hah!*

Jerry could easily become her boyfriend if she wasn't careful. This was supposed to be a temporary deal. She just needed enough money to get her own place. She'd have to stand firm. But god! How he made her feel! He had been so patient, giving her an orgasm before he did anything for himself. And when he entered her, she had come so close to another orgasm, she didn't want him to stop. Thank god he did or she might be pregnant right now!

He promised to buy condoms. She knew they'd fuck again. And she had a very strong suspicion that she'd come. And come.

Which might screw up her plans to remain independent. She'd have to try to keep her head on straight. Make him keep paying her, for one thing. It was a small thing, but it helped keep the act in perspective. It was all she had.

\* \* \*

For the next week, Jerry didn't want to share Melissa with anyone. He still got his blow jobs on Mondays and Thursdays, but on Wednesday and again Saturday, they had sex. And he had bought condoms, so he didn't have to interrupt their love-making. And that's what it was to Jerry – love-making. Not fucking.

Each time, she made him pay her thirty bucks and she'd hand it over later as if it had come from another source. He went along with the charade although he didn't completely agree with it. Seemed like a lot of trouble.

Jerry made sure their love-making sessions were just as much about her as him. She came twice the second time they made love and three times the third time, thanks to the condoms. They helped reduce the sensations and normally he hated them but in this case, they helped keep him from coming too soon. But he still wanted her on the pill. Eventually, he wanted the right to fuck her bareback. He wasn't yet sure if she'd go along with it.

By Saturday, Melissa was bugging him to find her a customer.

"Come on, Jerry, we can't go on like this. Either I'm going to make some real money, or I'm going to shoot myself. I can't stand feeling so useless."

"It's a big step. I just wanted to make sure you were ready."

"After fucking you all week, I think I'm ready for anyone."

That gave him pause. "Are you going to fuck

someone right away?"

"No, actually, I want to start with blow jobs, work my way up, once I get my nerve."

"That's probably wise." If he had his way, she'd only give blow jobs. It maintained the illusion that she was his exclusive property.

"So, you know of anyone?"

"Yeah, actually I do." Frank would probably jump at the chance. "I'm just not sure how to approach him."

"Just give it to him straight. You've got a horny girl at home who's dying to suck cock. How hard could it be?"

"Well, uh… I kinda told him you were my girlfriend."

"What? Why'da do that?"

"I guess I was bragging or something. Or hoping."

"You're going to have to straighten him out. He won't want anything to do with me if he thinks I'm yours."

"Yeah. Don't worry, I'll figure it out."

"Good. I'd like to start Monday or Tuesday. Can you set something up?"

"How much do you think you should charge?"

"I dunno – twenty dollars?"

"Let's make it thirty and see how he reacts. We can always lower it later. But it's hard to raise it."

"Okay, whatever you say. You're the pimp."

"Yeah, great."

On Sunday, he begged her to make love but she resisted. "No, you're getting too attached," she told him. "Besides, I don't want to be sore for my first customer."

"But you said you were only going to give blow jobs!"

"I know, but I want to be ready in case they make me an offer I can't refuse."

Her cool approach to her newfound profession impressed him, although he didn't want to admit it. She certainly seemed to have a level head on her shoulders, more so than he did.

Monday, he found himself painting doors with Frank and trying to broach the subject. Humor seemed to be the most direct route.

"Hey, Frank," he said. "Do you know why a bride smiles when she's walking down the aisle?"

"Uh, okay – I don't know, why?"

"She knows she's given her last blow job."

Frank chuckled. "Yeah, that's about right."

"What – that lovely wife of yours won't do it?"

"Not for about ten years. But we've been married for fourteen, so I guess I can't complain too much."

"Come on, that's tragic."

He laughed. "I doubt she even remembers how to do it."

"You ever go out and find a girl who would?"

"You mean, cheat on my wife? I'm shocked, shocked, I tell you," he said, quoting the famous line from 'Casablanca.'

"Ohh, you have, you dog you."

He grinned. "Shhh. I'm not telling. You're inferring."

"What would you pay to get a blow job from a

cute eighteen-year-old?"

He stopped painting and turned. "What?"

"An eighteen-year-old who gives great blow jobs. And I know, because I've had some."

"You really know someone like that?"

"Yes I do. And she's looking for some discreet customers. Very discreet."

"How much?"

"Thirty bucks."

"Thirty? I can get them for twenty downtown."

"Ohh, so you have tried them out, eh?"

"A man needs a good blow job once in a while, I won't deny it. And if the wife won't do it…" he trailed off.

"But those gals for twenty – I'll bet they didn't look like a cute cheerleader."

"No, they looked a bit weather-beaten, I admit. So who do you know like that?"

"Remember Melissa? On the cheerleading squad?"

"The one who broke her ankle before state? *That* Melissa?"

"Yep."

"And she's giving blow jobs now?"

"It's only temporary. She's been looking for a job for a couple months and is desperate."

"How do you know her so well?"

"She's an orphan, you know and she's been having trouble finding a place to stay. The group home kicked her out when she turned eighteen. So I let her stay in my spare bedroom."

"Hey, this is the girl you were telling me about! You were in love or something!"

"Yes and no. I was smitten, I admit, but she doesn't want anything to do with an old man like me."

"Hell, I'm older than you are."

"Yeah, but for business, it's okay. She wants to keep it just business between us now."

"And she's willing to ... do that for me while you're around? That's cold, man."

"I know, it's not perfect. But she's desperate to move out and get her own place and she needs a few extra bucks. And I'm kinda stuck too. It would be best if she left, but I can't toss her out – I'm not that cruel." He paused. "This was all her idea, you know."

"Really? Prostitution? She's a fool."

"I know. I mean in the long run, she would be. But if she can get out quickly, she might be okay."

Frank gave him a flat look. "And how many girls do you know get out quickly?"

"She's still looking for a regular job. This is just to make some short-term money."

"Thirty bucks, huh?"

"No one can ever know. It would have to be a big secret."

"It's not like I'm going to talk about it. Jeez, Jerry."

"I know. I just felt I had to say it."

"Yeah, yeah, I get it." He thought about it as he painted the last part of the door. Finally he turned. "Well, hell, for thirty bucks, I might try her out. But she'd better be good!"

"Oh, she is, trust me."

"When?"

Jerry thought about his own blow job that awaited

him that afternoon. "Uh, tomorrow?"

"Okay. But this better be on the up and up. You're not scamming me, are you?"

Jerry raised his right hand. "I swear."

"Okay."

When he arrived home, Melissa was sitting on the couch, watching TV. He said, "I've got you a customer."

She turned, her eyes wide. "Really?"

"Yep. Frank, my buddy at work. He's coming by tomorrow for a BJ."

"What time?"

"After work."

"And he agreed to the price?"

"He thought it was a bit high, but when I told him it was a cute cheerleader, he went for it."

"You didn't tell him who I was, did you?" She looked horrified.

"He knows you, Mel. He's been a janitor at the school longer than I have. I'm sure you've seen him around."

"Ohh, right, that older guy."

"He's only forty-five."

"Well, that's old to me. Hmm. I'm not sure I like it that he knows me and everything."

"He's very discreet. He won't say anything. Besides, he's married – he'd be in more trouble than you if he got caught."

"He's married?! How can he do that?"

"Oh, Mel, you've got a lot to learn about men and marriage. The thing is, most wives stop giving blow jobs after the wedding. But men really like them. So what are they gonna do, just do without for the rest of their lives? Not hardly."

"Gee, I wonder if wives realize that."

"I'm sure they do and probably don't care. In fact, if you polled wives everywhere, a good percentage wouldn't begrudge their husbands an occasional BJ now and then from someone else – as long as they weren't fucking her."

"Really? That's sad."

"Marriage can be sad sometimes."

"You sound like you've been married before."

"No, I just hang around with married men and hear their stories."

"So… tomorrow, huh? I guess this is real now."

"Yep."

"You know I'm just going to give you that money. Maybe you should give him the BJ."

"Oh, thanks a lot. But look, I can't take all of it. I'm supposed to be helping you. How about if we split it, fifty-fifty? That way, you'll have some walking around money."

She nodded. "Okay! That sounds fair. Thanks, Jerry. You're really being great about this. I know you'd prefer to keep me to yourself."

He shrugged. "Yeah, I know. But you've made your position clear. I understand it."

"Thanks." She got up from the couch and came up to him. "Well, I guess I'd better practice, huh?"

"Got that right." He unzipped his pants.

Melissa dropped to her knees in front of him and looked up adoringly. "I'm going to practice my techniques, try to make you feel special. So try not to laugh, okay?"

"Oh, I won't laugh. Trust me. But you're going to have to take off your T-shirt."

She nodded and quickly stripped it off. She wasn't wearing a bra underneath and her perky breasts made his cock swell even more. She eased it out and began to tongue it. He hadn't even showered and she didn't seem to mind.

"I'm probably a bit sweaty," he cautioned.

"I know. But Frank will be too and he won't be showering first, so I might as well get used to it." She took him inside her mouth and he stopped talking.

The blow job was excellent. She knew how to tease him and bring him right to the edge and back off, keeping him on his tiptoes and well inside the pleasure zone. When she began to speed up, he grabbed the back of her head and forced himself down her throat and began squirting great gobs of his seed. She took it all in like a pro.

When she pulled back, gasping, she looked up at him and smiled. "How was that?" she asked, her mouth still sticky white. She rolled it around with her tongue and swallowed again.

"Oh, honey, Frank is going to die. He won't believe it can be so good."

"Um. Is he big? Like bigger than you?" She stood up and helped ease Jerry's cock back into his pants and zipped him up.

"Hell, I don't know," he laughed. "We don't exactly shower together."

"Oh. I thought maybe you did. Or something."

"No, you'll just have to be surprised."

"Okay."

"So what are you going to wear tomorrow?"

"Uh, I don't know – does it matter?"

"I like the idea of a T-shirt without a bra. It will drive him wild, even if you don't take your shirt off. Your nipples will really stick out against the fabric."

"Oh, okay. I can do that. I thought you meant I should put on a dress or something."

"That's for later, when you want to offer men the complete 'girlfriend experience'."

She looked puzzled. "What's that?"

"You don't know? It's all the rage nowadays. A prostitute pretends she's a guy's girlfriend for the evening. That includes dinner, maybe a dance or two. He wants to show you off. Then later, he'll fuck your brains out. You can make really good money."

"Really? Like how much?"

"I don't know for sure. I only know what I read about in the papers and such. But I've heard it can be a couple thousand a night."

"Really? That would be great!"

"But you'd have to look the part from head to toe. And act the part."

"Sounds intriguing."

"Do some research on the Internet. You'll be amazed." He paused. "It means, of course, you'd be a full-fledged pro. No simple blow jobs. You'd have to really get into the fucking and all that."

"Yeah. I don't think I'm ready. Not yet, anyway."

"Are you still going to look for work?"

"Yeah, I guess." She didn't sound enthusiastic.

"Okay. I'll go see what we have for dinner."

"No, no," she said, putting up her hand. "You go shower and relax. Have a beer. I'll cook tonight. It's the least I can do."

"You're like the perfect wife, you know that?"

She smiled. "Thanks. Now go."

He went into the bathroom and took a long, hot shower. He felt very good, considering his sometime girlfriend was about to blow his co-worker. And he had set it up! The whole thing was surreal.

No, he reminded himself. She's not your girlfriend and never was. She's just an orphan kid who needed a place to stay for a while. It might have been better if he'd never offered to put her up. But that's not what his cock was telling him.

Frank was nervous. "Are you sure this is on the up and up?" he asked as the afternoon waned and his "appointment" approached.

"Yes, Frank, relax. It's a simple BJ. Don't make a big deal out of it."

"Yeah, well, you're not married. I mean, besides the guilt I have to deal with, I have to worry about getting caught – or blackmailed. You wouldn't blackmail me, wouldja?"

Jerry laughed. "Oh yeah, I really want to tap into the vast Sawyer fortune. Jeez, Frank, you don't' make enough money to bother with, even if I was that kind of person."

"So why exactly are you doing this again? I understand why she's doing it, but I don't quite get why you're being her pimp."

"I want her to move out in order to keep my sanity. This seems to be the only way to do it, unless she finds a real job."

"I don't know man, this could blow up in your face."

"Tell me about it."

"Okay. It's your funeral. But if you get caught, don't tell anyone about me."

"I won't."

Jerry left a few minutes before four to make sure Melissa was ready for him. Frank would drive over later.

"If anyone asks, I'm just having a beer with you. That's what I told Debbie," Frank told him as he headed for the parking lot.

"Gotcha," Jerry said, trying not to roll his eyes.

At home, Jerry found Melissa was pacing the living room. She looked like a wet dream in her shorts and a pink Hello Kitty T-shirt. It was obvious she wasn't wearing a bra. She looked up as soon as he entered. "Is he here?"

"No, but he'll be here soon. You all set?" He couldn't stop himself from thumbing a nipple through the material.

She shied away. "I guess. I'm as nervous as a cat!"

"Try to relax. Pretend it's me you're blowing and you'll do fine."

"Yeah, but it won't be you. What if he's too big? What if I can't get him to come? What if he refuses to pay me?"

"Stop worrying, it won't help. You wanted this, now you've got it. Maybe you'd just as soon go back to looking for a regular job and forget all this."

"No, no, I've looked until I'm blue in the face. I just need to make a few bucks, that's all. This isn't my chosen profession."

"Uh huh." Jerry wasn't sure he believed her. He knew, once she started making money, it would be very hard to stop.

They both heard the car pull into the driveway and Melissa gave Jerry a frightened look before squaring her shoulders and trying to get herself under control. "I can't believe I'm actually doing this," she muttered.

"I can't either," he said as he went to the door.

"Hey, Frank!" He greeted his friend. "Long time no see."

Frank laughed nervously. "Yeah."

"Come in, come in. Can I get you a beer?"

"Uh, no, not right now." His eyes were locked onto Melissa, who stood nervously in the living room.

"Frank, this is Melissa. Mel, Frank."

"Jesus, Jerry – I should probably use another name, don't you think?" Mel said.

"Hell," he told her. "You know his name, right?"

"Yeah. I guess."

Frank smiled. "It doesn't matter." He stepped forward. "I remember you from school. You are as cute as a bug."

"Uh, thanks, I guess. You're pretty cute yourself."

Frank tipped his head. "Aw, no way. I'm an old man by your standards."

"No, I mean... Hell, I don't know what I mean."

Jerry jumped in before the conversation could go sideways. "So, everyone's agreed on the price?"

"Uh huh," Jerry said. "Thirty bucks, right?"

"Right," Melissa responded. She bit her lower lip. "I, uh, guess we should get started, huh?"

"Where?" Frank looked around. "Not here, I hope."

"No, in my bedroom. We'll have some privacy."

Frank glanced at Jerry. "You sure you're okay with this?"

Jerry nodded. "Yeah, I'm okay."

"Okay," Frank told her, "lead the way."

She headed down the hallway, Frank right behind. He turned and gave Jerry a look and bit his knuckle as if to say, "Wow!"

Jerry went into the kitchen and grabbed a beer. He leaned against the counter and tried not to listen, but the walls were thin and he could hear the murmur of their voices. Jerry closed his eyes and tried not to imagine what was happening, which proved to be impossible. He had felt the girl's lips on his cock and he knew Frank was in heaven right about now.

\* \* \*

"You are so damn cute! I never thought I'd get a blow job from such a cute girl!"

"Uh, yeah. This is just temporary. Until I can find a regular job. You know how it is out there." She felt jumpy and tried to calm her nerves.

"Yeah, I hear ya, honey." He looked her up and down. "So, how do you want to do this?"

"Maybe we should get the money out of the way first."

"Oh, sure." He handed a wadded up twenty and a ten.

It disappeared into her pants. "You want to sit down?"

"Uh, yeah, I guess I do. It's been so long, I've forgotten how I like it." He sat on the edge of the bed and seemed jumpy as well.

"Your wife doesn't do this for you anymore?"

"Hell no."

Melissa knelt between his legs and began to unbuckle his pants. His cock was only semi-hard. She worried that maybe she didn't look pretty enough, despite what he had said. She began to tease his cock with her fingers. It hardly budged.

"Sorry," he said. "I'm a little nervous."

"Really? I'm nervous too."

"That's actually good. I mean, if we both feel the same, we can work through it."

She smiled. "Yeah, sure we can." She leaned down and kissed the tip of his cock. It swelled a little and it encouraged her.

"You know what would help?"

She looked up. "What?"

"If you took off your T-shirt. I know I'd get excited, looking at your breasts."

Melissa nodded and quickly stripped it off. "But nothing else."

"Okay, that's okay."

His hand reached out and caressed the side of her breast and immediately his cock swelled to near full height. "See?" He grinned.

She nodded. "I do see." She took the tip into his mouth and licked the shaft. It wasn't too big for her and she was at least grateful for that.

"Oh yeah! Oh yeah!"

Nothing more was said for several minutes.

* * *

"Oh yeah! Oh yeah!" The decibel level increased another notch and it was obvious Frank was about done. Jerry drained his beer.

"Oh god! Sweet jesus!"

Silence fell. Apparently, it was over. The voices returned to a murmur and Jerry went into the living room to wait. Frank came out a few minutes later, looking pleased with himself. He came in and said, "Now, how about that beer?"

Jerry pointed to the kitchen. He felt strangely numb now that it was over. "Help yourself."

Frank found himself one and twisted off the cap. Jerry heard him toss it into the trash can. His eyes were locked on the doorway down the hall. Frank came out just as Melissa stepped out into the hall. He raised his beer in tribute and Mel looked embarrassed and disappeared into the bathroom. Frank joined him on the couch.

"Wow," he said. "Thanks."

"Worth the money?"

"Oh yeah!"

"Wanna repeat? Say next week?"

"Oh, hell, I would love it – but I can't. I only have so much spending money each week. The rest goes into the joint account. I can't be dipping into that too often. Maybe the week after?"

Jerry nodded. "You know of anyone else who might like to get a BJ from such a cute girl?"

"Yeah – my next-door neighbor, Stu. He's always

going on about his fat wife who has decided she hates sex. As if anyone would want to fuck that broad. But he'd rather get laid, to tell you the truth. At least, that's what he tells me."

"She's working up to it, but she's not ready. Can't force these things."

"I hear ya. I'll ask him – I think a BJ might do for now. Better than nothing."

"Can he be discreet?"

Frank shrugged. "Sure."

"We should probably come up with a new name for her. She's right about not using her real name with the johns that don't know her from school."

"Yeah. What do you think? Brandy? Candy? Lila?" Frank offered.

"I don't know. Maybe Mel has some ideas."

Melissa came out and stood at the end of the hall, as if debating whether to join the men. She seemed ill at ease. Jerry tried to break the tension.

"Hey, Mel, if you were to come up with a name for you, what would it be?"

"I dunno."

"How about Brandy?" Frank asked.

She made a face. "Sounds too whore-ish."

Frank gave Jerry a sideways glance as if to say, "So?" To Mel, he said. "Well, you should come up with something."

"I kinda like the name Jami, with an 'i'."

"Hey, that's pretty good," Frank told her.

"Yeah, I like it. Okay, you're Jami from now on – professionally," Jerry said.

"Okay." She fidgeted. "Well, I'm going to my

room and rest for a bit."

"Okay," Jerry told her. She disappeared and closed the door behind her.

Frank looked at his watch. "Well, I'd better go. Don't want to get into trouble." He drained his beer and stood up. "Thanks, and I mean it, Jerry. She was great."

"Good. And have Stu call me to set something up."

"I will."

After Frank left, Jerry went down the hall and knocked on her door. "It's okay, he's gone."

The door opened a crack. "Really? I felt so awkward, afterwards. I didn't really want to come out and chat him up. It seemed wrong somehow."

"I understand. You did fine." He hesitated. "So, how was it? Do you feel okay?"

"You mean, did I freak out? No. Thankfully, it went very, uh, smoothly. He seemed very grateful."

"Good. And you got the money?"

"Oh yeah! I owe you some of it." She pulled a few bills out of her pocket. "I've only got a twenty and a ten. Do you have a five?"

Jerry found a five in his wallet and she gave him the twenty. She put the rest in her pants and patted it. "Well, there it is – my first earnings as a whore. My mom, whoever she was, would've been so proud," she said sarcastically.

"What did happen to you – do you know? I mean, do you know why you were put up for adoption?"

"No and now that I'm eighteen, I hope to find out. But I can guess – I'd say she was a kid who couldn't handle a baby. You know the story."

"Yeah. Speaking of which, we got to get you to the doctor, get you on the pill – just in case, you know. You'll have to make sure everyone wears condoms."

"Like you did that time?" She grinned when she said it.

"Yeah, that was kind of a close call, wasn't it? But it felt good, that's for sure."

"Yeah, I don't like condoms as much. I don't know why."

"Hey, you and I can make a deal – once you're on the pill, we'll make love without them, okay? That way, we both get the pleasure."

She tipped her head sideways. "I don't know – I don't want you falling for me or anything. This is all just temporary."

"I know it – and I'm not sure I want to run a brothel out of my house."

"Yeah."

After dinner, while they were watching TV, Jerry's cell phone rang. It was a number he didn't recognize. He muted the show and answered it.

"Hello?"

"Yeah, is this Jerry?"

"Uh, yeah, who is this?"

"Stu, Frank's friend." The voice was a whisper, as if he was trying not to let anyone hear his side of the conversation.

"Oh!" He sat up. Mel shot him a glance.

"Frank tells me you got a girl – barely legal – who gives, uh, well, you know. I'm not sure I should say over the phone."

"Yes, it's true. You wanna come by, say tomorrow or Friday?"

"It's thirty, right?"

"Yes."

"And if things go okay, there might be more, uh, options, later?"

"Yes, that's right. It's all brand new right now."

"Okay, let's do it tomorrow. I can't wait."

Jerry gave him the address and they set the time for four thirty. He hung up. Melissa was staring at him with big eyes.

"Your second customer."

"Jeez. I didn't know there were that many horny middle-aged guys around here."

"Oh, you'd be surprised."

Melissa was still nervous the next morning. "God, what if he's horribly ugly or fat? I don't know if I could do it."

"Well, that could be a problem in your chosen profession," Jerry told her. "Most of the customers who go to pros aren't really dateable. At least, that's how I figure it. I could be wrong."

"Yeah, that makes sense. God."

"Well, I gotta get to work. You doing anything special today?"

"No. I mean, I'll clean up and stuff, but otherwise, I'll just sit around and wait for my customer, I guess. God, I can't believe I'm doing this."

"Hey, you can quit anytime."

"No I can't. I've got to earn my own money – you know that – and the job market sucks."

"Okay. Well, bye." He kissed her on the cheek.

She gave him a big hug that made him hard and said, "Hurry home, dear."

"Sure."

When he spotted Frank, his co-worker gave him a thumbs up. "Hey, did Stu call?"

"Yep. He's coming over today."

"Wow, that's great. I told him about the current rule, you know – only BJs. But I know he wants the real thing."

"I know – he told me. I said, 'soon.' That's about the best I can do. It's up to her."

"Yeah. She was great. She really knows what she's doing, doesn't she? I'm surprised – she's so young and all."

"She had a boyfriend she kept happy that way. But they broke up."

"Too bad for him."

"But good for us."

"So is she slipping your freebies?" He wiggled his eyebrows and winked.

"Sure. I'm the pimp, after all."

"You lucky dog!" Then he stopped. "Hey, wait a minute – are you taking a cut?"

"Oh no," he lied. "This is her 'get my own place' fund. But she does help out buying groceries and such."

"Huh."

"So you want a repeat when you get your next paycheck?"

"Ohh yeah. But I might be interested in the other, you know. When she's ready."

"That would be a lot more expensive."

"Yeah – what do you think she'd charge for the real deal?"

"I don't know – we haven't discussed it. But I'm thinking, for a sweet young pussy like that, it'd have to go for at least a hundred," Jerry told him.

"Jeez, that's pretty rich for my blood. I mean, she's probably worth it and all, but man…"

"I know, but she can't be giving it away free. The more she makes now, the sooner she can get her own place."

"Yeah, she could set up shop there. Might be the best thing for you, huh?"

"Yeah. I won't have to be around her when she's doing her thing."

Frank nodded sympathetically. "That bugging you?"

"Sure. I mean, I liked this girl. I can't help it if I'm too old for her."

"I know man, that sucks."

"Not to mention that if I get caught, I'd lose my job."

"That's for sure. The district frowns on the exploitation of young students."

"Former student," he reminded him. "And I'm not exploiting her – she's exploiting herself. But yeah, you're right."

When Jerry arrived home at four-twenty, he found a man sitting in his car at the curb. He went to the window and said, "Stu, right?"

The man nodded. "Yeah. You must be Jerry,

Frank's friend." Stu was a heavyset man about Frank's age, maybe a bit older. He had on a green Hawaiian shirt and shorts. He stuck out a hand.

"Yeah," Jerry responded, shaking it. "Give me a few minutes to prep the girl and then come up."

Stu nodded and Jerry went up the walk, marveling at how easy things were going. Well, business-wise, he mused. The emotional part was still hard for him. It helped to compartmentalize his feelings about Melissa. She wasn't interested in him so he should simply look at her as a business opportunity. She owed him, so why not?

Inside, Mel was watching TV. He felt an irrational flash of irritation at her, thinking she should still be looking for work. Even if she had been "everywhere" as she had told him, she should still keep looking. Did she really want to be a prostitute instead? There must be something wrong with her. It made it easier to think of her as a product he was selling.

"Mel, Stu's here. Are you ready?"

She glanced at her watch. "Already? He's early."

"I know. He can't wait. Do you need to freshen up?"

"No, I took a shower and all earlier. Besides, I'm only blowing him, right?"

"Right. But he wants more. He may ask how much you're gonna charge for a fuck – have you thought about it?"

"Uh… not really."

"I know we gotta get you to the doc first, but we should come up with a number for those who want it. I'd say at least a hundred."

"Really? That much?"

"It's not that much when you consider you're a fresh young thing, tight and cute. You could try to go for one-fifty."

"You think so? Wow."

"If he asks, tell him you're not sure you'd want to do that and when he presses, like I know he will, tell him one-fifty and see his reaction. If he jumps at it, we're charging too little. We might be able to get two hundred."

"Okay. You're the pimp."

"Just be sure and get the money up front."

The doorbell rang and Jerry let Stu in. He barely glanced at Jerry – all his attention was focused on Melissa, sitting on the couch. She rose and Jerry could see she was nervous.

"Jami, this is Stu; Stu, Jami."

"Shit, I shouldn't've used my real name," Stu blurted. "You're not going to get me into trouble, are you?"

"No, no I won't," she said. "I'll call you Sam, okay? I've already forgotten about the other name."

"Good. That's good." He paused and bit his lip. "So, how's this gonna work?" He shot a glance at Jerry.

"You go into the bedroom with M—I mean, Jami, pay her upfront and get ready for a great BJ. That's it."

"Okay."

Mel smiled at him and tipped her head. "Come on, Sam."

"Right." He followed her down the hall like a

puppy.

Jerry heard the door closed and could picture in his mind the scene there: Stu with his pants down around his ankles while Mel, kneeling before him, sucked on his hard cock until he spewed. He gave an involuntary shudder and went into the kitchen. He could hear the faint sounds and turned on the water to drown them out.

God, what was he doing? He knew his dick was talking again, telling him it was okay to risk his career – ha, some career! – for this piece of ass. But he really wanted to fuck her again, just a few more times. Once she got on the pill and made a few bucks, he'd pull the plug on all this. His head would have to override his cock. It was as simple as that.

He heard a distant bellow and he turned off the water. Silence descended over the house. He grabbed a beer and waited. Soon, Stu appeared in the doorway with a big smile on his face and said to Jerry, "Next week?"

Jerry nodded.

"For the real thing?"

"Uh, not sure about that. But for another BJ, if you want."

"Well, what's the holdup?"

"She's just a kid, you see. She has to work her way into it. If you rush her, she may just quit."

"Oh, okay. We wouldn't want that!" He winked and left, closing the door quietly behind him.

Jerry waited in the living room for Mel to come out. She went directly into the bathroom and closed the door. He could hear her brushing her teeth and gargling with mouthwash. She wasn't a very good whore if she had to do that every time. But it probably meant she was swallowing regularly now. That was good.

She came out and gave him a sheepish look. "Uh, hi."

"How did it go?"

"It went fine. Oh!" She came forward and handed him fifteen dollars. "Your cut."

"Did you talk about prices?"

"Oh! Yes. He was really anxious to fuck me. Made me feel a little creepy. I said I wasn't ready and all and he kept after me, touching me and everything. So I told him two hundred and you know what? He hardly batted an eye. He said, 'Just say when.' He wanted to do it right then! But I wouldn't let him."

"Okay, that's it. Tomorrow you need to go down to the free clinic. You want me to go with you?" He really didn't want to, but thought she might need moral support.

"No, that's okay, I'm eighteen, I'm supposed to be all independent now. It's on the bus route, right?"

"Right." He gave her the address and she promised she'd go in the morning.

"I guess this is getting real, huh?"

"It's a risky move, but very lucrative. If you don't feel like doing it, don't do it. You can mess up your mind otherwise."

"I'm just going to do it for a while, that's all."

Neither one spoke for a bit.

"Well, I guess I'd better start dinner."

"Sure, if you're up for it. I can cook, you know."

"I know. I just want to help out." She went into the kitchen.

Jerry followed her. "Hey, tomorrow's Thursday, what do you say we practice, you know?"

"Huh?"

"Making love. To get you ready for Stu and the others."

"You mean fucking, don't you?"

"Well, yeah, but I was trying to be polite."

"You don't have to be polite around me. I know what I'm doing. At least, I think I do."

"Okay. So whaddya say?"

"Let me think about it. I'll tell you after I visit the clinic."

# Chapter Eight

Jerry was eager to get home Thursday. He hoped Mel had decided to "practice" with him. The more he could fuck her, the better he felt about letting her stay. At least, that's what he told himself. His heart seemed to tell time something different, but he managed to ignore it.

He came in to find her sitting on the couch, as usual, watching TV. He said, "Well, how did it go?"

She turned off the tube and grimaced. "It was okay. I don't like those exams."

"You mean, pelvics?"

"Yeah. The doctor was an old man who smelled of cigarette smoke. Can you imagine? A doctor who smokes?"

"He must be old school." He hurried on. "So, did you get your pills?"

"Oh, no – he gave me a shot. Depro- something."

"Really? What's that do?"

"He said I'd be protected for three months."

His heart – and his cock – leapt. "Really?"

"That's what he said. But he told me to wear condoms for a week or so."

"Aww."

"Just to be sure, you know. You wouldn't want to knock me up, would you?"

"No." It sounded to Jerry like she had made her decision about fucking him. "So, can we? It *is* Thursday, you know."

"Yeah, I guess. I've been thinking about it – I can make so much more money if I start fucking guys instead of just blowing them. I mean, two hundred a fuck vs. thirty a BJ? It's no contest."

"Yeah, except you aren't charging me," he pointed out. "I mean, not really."

"Oh, I know. You're a special case – you're my pimp. Besides, you've put up with me when no one else would. I owe you."

*Got that right*, he thought.

"Okay, then. Let's go!"

"Don't you want to take a shower first? I did."

"Oh, right. Sorry." He hurried into the bathroom and took a quick shower. When he came out, he didn't bother with clothes. Melissa was already in her bed, naked, waiting for him.

"Oh, god," he breathed when he caught sight of her.

She grinned and pointed at his hard cock. "Somebody is happy to see me."

"Wait! I've got to get the condoms." He practically ran down the hall to his bedroom and found a condom in the nightstand. He came back, tearing off the wrapper as he went, and jumped on the bed. Mel giggled and pretended to try and escape. He grabbed her and she squealed in mock horror.

He slipped under the covers and began to kiss her

all over.

"Ohhh, I like this part," she breathed.

He made sure she was fully aroused before he entered her. He knew he should go down on her but he couldn't wait. He slipped the condom on and crawled between her legs. She put a hand out on his chest to stop him.

"What?"

"Is this how it will be? With the others, I mean? Like Stu?"

"Probably not. Well, some of them might want to take their time, really get into it. But others will just want to slip it in and come right away. You might have to use some KY jelly or something if you aren't aroused enough."

"Eww."

"I know. They can't all be gentle like me."

"You're sweet."

*Now shut up*, he felt like saying, but he waited until her legs relaxed and he eased the tip of his cock into her wetness. And she was wet, that much he could tell through the latex. Slowly, he pressed more of himself into her and watched her eyes widen.

"Ohhh, Jerry."

"Let me know if I hurt you."

"No, it feels good. You're going slow. That's nice."

He fought his impatience and began to slowly move his cock back and forth, pressing a fraction of an inch more into her with each forward thrust. She was starting to get into it, he could tell. Her breathing shallowed and her mouth came open.

"Uh, uh, uh." She started making noises in time

with his tiny thrusts.

Jerry kept pressing until his cock disappeared inside her. When he was fully seated, he stopped and gazed into her eyes.

"You all right?"

"Yeah. It feels good."

"It will feel better when we don't have to use condoms."

"Uh huh."

He pulled out and pressed himself all the way back in. Her eyes widened and she made a small moan in her throat. That was all the encouragement he needed – he began to fuck her in earnest now, thrusting hard with each inward stroke.

"Oh god!" She gasped and threw her head back.

Jerry was a machine now, thrusting and grunting as his hands gripped her shoulders. He wanted to get his cock as far into her as he possibly could, as if to plant his seed deep within her womb. The condom actually helped desensitize his cock so he could thrust longer, harder. Mel was a rag doll on the bed, rocking in time with him, her hands grabbing his biceps for support, her legs wrapped around his hips.

With a bellow, he came at last and she shuddered and held him close. Jerry wasn't sure if she came and realized it was a teaching moment. They collapsed together and when their breathing had eased, he propped himself up on one elbow.

"Hey, that was great. Did you come?"

"Uh, no. I guess I was a bit nervous or something."

"That's okay, but when you're with a customer, you've gotta fake it."

"Why? What does he care as long as he gets off?"

"Because it's part of the fantasy, you see. He wants to feel like the macho man, making the woman come and all. So you have to act like it was the best sex you've ever had."

"Even if it sucked?"

"Especially if it sucked. If you don't make him feel good, he won't come back. And regulars are what will make or break your business."

"Oh. Really?"

"It makes sense, doesn't it? You don't want to fuck a new guy every time, do you? And if you do, you only increase the chances one of them will be a cop."

"God, you must think I'm so naïve. I never even thought of that."

"You should. What you're doing is illegal."

"I know."

"Okay, lesson's over. Now I want to make you come."

"Really?" She dimpled. "You don't have to."

"I want to."

He went down on her, pushing her pubic hair out of the way to expose her clit, which was standing at attention. He began to tongue it, gently at first and then harder until she was shuddering.

"Oh god."

He teased her, alternating between the tip and the flat of his tongue until she was shaking. When she finally crested over the top into her orgasm, her body shook with the pleasure of it.

"OH MY GOD! OH SHIT!"

Jerry grinned and pulled back. Let her want to

leave him now, he thought. She won't be getting this kind of loving anywhere else. Even as he thought it, he knew he was being foolish. She was just a fresh-faced whore.

Which reminded him.

He waited until she calmed down and leaned on his elbow next to her. "Thanks."

"No, thank you! That was… well, it was amazing."

"Did you get a chance to look into the 'girlfriend experience'?" he asked.

"Oh! Yes, I did. I looked it up online. I was amazed!"

"It's all the rage, apparently. There are a lot of rich, lonely guys out there."

"Right! I could make good money. I mean, really good."

"Yeah? Did you find prices?"

"Yeah, some. Girls are getting, like, three hundred bucks an hour! Wow!"

"I could give you some tips if you want to try that. Probably not right now, but later, maybe."

"Tips?"

"Uh huh. Things men expect from those escort models or whatever you call them."

"Really? How do you know about this?"

"Uh, just from reading – I haven't hired one, if that's what you're thinking. You know I couldn't afford it."

Melissa smiled. "And I don't think you'd need to. You're a sweet guy, I'm sure there are girls out there who won't mind if you're a janitor."

"Maybe not. But we were talking about you."

"Okay, Mr. Expert: What would I have to do to make those big bucks?"

Jerry sat up and ticked the points off his fingers. "One, you should lighten your hair. Blondes really do have more fun – and they make more money."

"Well, that's easy enough."

"Two, you'd have to shave... down there." He pointed.

Her eyes went wide. "Really?"

"Oh yes. More girls are doing that anyway, aren't they?"

"I guess. I know I saw a lot of girls doing it in high school. They said it was no different than shaving under their arms, but I thought it made them look like little girls again."

"That's the point – men love the fantasy without risking arrest. Besides, it makes it easier for them to go down on you."

"Oh? Did you have some trouble just now?"

He grinned. "Not really. But it would be nicer if it was smooth."

"Huh."

"Something to think about."

"Sure."

He glanced at the clock on the nightstand. "Well, guess it's time to make dinner."

"Okay. Let me freshen up and I'll be right out."

He took that as his clue to leave. He went out and starting pulling out ingredients. He heard her go into the bathroom and close the door. A moment later, the shower went on. He focused on his task and tried not to think about her slender young body in the shower.

It wasn't easy. His cock, although thoroughly satiated, half-swelled in response and he shook his head and muttered to himself.

Mel came out later and joined in and they had dinner on the table in no time.

"I think I'm gonna do it," she said as they ate.

"Do what, exactly?"

"The girlfriend experience stuff."

"Do you know what to do? I mean, that's beyond me, you know. You'd have to find an escort agency."

"I know. That part scares me a little. I like to be independent. Can I stay here a little while longer so I can get my nerve up?"

"Sure. As long as I'm getting laid regularly, I'm fine with it." He wasn't sure it that was true, but it sounded right. What man wouldn't want a live-in whore?

She made a face. "Okay, but don't fall in love or anything."

"I won't."

Of course, it was easier said than done. Jerry wanted to sleep with her that night, but she politely but firmly rejected him, saying, "That's a habit I don't think we should get into, okay?"

"Okay," he said, feeling unwanted all over again. He went to his room and tried to sleep.

The next day, he told Frank about her plans, just to see what the older man thought.

"Oh man, you are getting in way too deep here, Jerry," he responded.

"Yeah, maybe I am."

"I mean, how long are you gonna let this girl use your house as her brothel? Don't you think she will start to draw attention to herself sooner or later?"

"Yeah, I'm hoping it can be discreet, you know, for the short term."

"Ha! Just wait until word gets out. You'll have men camped on your lawn, waiting their turn."

"You think?"

"Sure. How many guys like me, married forever, wouldn't jump at the chance to fuck an eighteen-year-old girl, especially one with a body like hers?"

"Just wait until I get her all fixed up."

"What do you mean?"

Jerry explained about having her lighten her hair and shave. Frank whistled. "Now you're making me horny all over again. Damn! How much is she gonna charge me for a fuck?"

"Well, I'm thinking we can get two hundred, at least. But maybe for you, one-fifty."

"One-fifty! Last week it was a hundred!"

"I know, I know. But she's trying to make as much money as she can in a very short time, before we have to pull the plug."

Frank laughed, a rich baritone. "You think she's gonna pull the plug after she starts making ten grand a month? You're dreaming. She's well on her way to becoming a real whore and you're just a sucker who is letting her stay in your place and practice!"

Jerry suddenly did feel exactly like that.

# Chapter Nine

"Okay, we're gonna change things around a little bit," he told her when he arrived home that afternoon.

She looked up from the couch. "Huh?"

"I'm risking my job here and once you're gone, all I'll have to show for it will be some memories – well, some memories and a few extra bucks. You'll forget all about me and if I ever called you up, you'd demand I pay top dollar, just like everyone else."

His intensity caught her off guard. "Where did this come from?"

"I've just been thinking," he responded, preferring to leave Frank out of it. "So things are going to change for the short term."

"What do you mean?"

"First of all, it means you're gonna fuck me whenever I want to, not on your schedule. And I won't be paying you any money, either. If you need spending money, just find more clients to take care of."

"But how can I find them? I'm relying on you for that."

"Oh, I'll still help, but I'm sure you can do your part, too. I'm not saying go around and post flyers, I'm just saying, flirt a little bit with some of the older men you come across. Like those managers of all those businesses you've applied to. Surely some of them tried to come onto you."

Mel made a face. "Yeah. Ick. Sure, I mean, at the time I was offended. I'm not sure I wanted to work at those places." She tipped her head. "I'm just not sure how to broach the subject of paying for it."

"Make it sound like a one-time deal. Like, go back to one of those places and tell him you're checking on job positions again and flirt a bit and see where it goes."

"Huh. I don't know…"

"Second, let's get your hair fixed. And the rest, too." He waved at hand at her groin.

"Well, I did trim it up a bit. But I couldn't bring myself to shave it all off."

"Why not?"

"That's like my mark of womanhood or something. You know, I'm finally eighteen and an adult – and now I'm supposed to go backward?"

"Don't think of it that way, think of it as a costume you're putting on. The blonde hair, the sexy talk and walk – you know the drill. Make men want you."

"I've never tried to lead guys on like that before."

"Well, it's time."

Melissa frowned. "So you must really want me out of here, huh?"

"No, no! I like it, actually. But it's still hard on me to hear you giving head. Think of how it will be when you start fucking guys. I'll feel like a chump."

"You'll never be a chump. I'm sorry I don't feel the same way toward you. Sometimes I wish I did – it would make things a lot easier. I could just live her and mooch off you. I mean, as long as I fucked your brains out, right?"

"Yeah. Which makes me wonder why you'd rather become a prostitute than hang around with me. Makes me feel kinda worthless."

She came to him at once. "Ohh, please don't feel that way. You've been wonderful. It's more about my independence than you. Can't you see the difference?"

"I guess." He shook his head. All his bluster had evaporated. "I'm sorry if I came on strong there. I'm a bit emotional about it."

"I can see that." She paused. "So when do you want to do this makeover?"

"This weekend would be fine. We can get one of those hair-color kits from the store and you can take care of the rest – unless you want me to do it."

"Oh, no, I can do it. I'm a bit afraid of letting you down there with a razor. What if you slipped up or something?" She shivered.

"Well, I wouldn't, but I can understand how you feel." He clapped his hands together. "Great! It's all worked out. Now, come on, I'm horny!"

"Again? Didn't you just get laid yesterday?"

"Yes, and I'll probably want to get laid again tomorrow. I mean, this is so temporary, I want to get what I can before it ends. I'm sure you know what a treat this is for me. It's not like I've had lots of women throw themselves at me."

She smiled. "Actually, the way you make love, it's a treat for me too."

"Good."

He took her hand and led her down the hall.

He made her come once before he entered her and did not use a condom this time. She didn't object. It felt wonderful to feel her softness against his cock and the muscles underneath that milked him for his seed. He managed to hold out until she crested into her second orgasm before he emptied himself into her. It was glorious.

Afterwards, as they lay in a sweaty heap, exhausted but happy, Jerry rolled over on his back and said, "Yeah, it was trimmed up, I could tell. But now it's time to shave it all off."

"You're sure about this?"

"I am. If you don't believe me, just check out some of the girls on the web lately. About ninety percent shave."

"Okay. I suppose if you're wrong, I can always grow it back."

"Right. But I'm not wrong."

Mel got up. "I guess there's no time like the present. I'm all sweaty anyway, might as well shower."

Jerry groaned. "Now you tell me! I'm just going to want to try you out as soon as you're done and I'm all used up!"

She laughed. "Too bad, big boy. You'll just have to wait." She slipped out of bed naked and headed for the door. He watched her cute butt wiggle and felt his cock bravely try to stiffen, to no avail.

"I must be getting old," he muttered.

He heard the shower go on and had a sudden urge to join her. He got up and crossed the hall to the bathroom door. Shit! It was locked. She must've anticipated he might try it and didn't want him there while she shaved. Too bad.

He padded naked into the kitchen and poured himself an iced tea. He leaned against the counter and mentally pictured Melissa in the shower stall, washing up, spreading that lather all over her cute young body, then reaching for the razor…

His cock swelled a bit more.

He smiled down at it. "You just keep trying, little buddy."

When he heard the shower turn off thirty minutes later, he was at half-staff. Just thinking what she might look like now excited him. The bathroom door clicked open and he stepped out into the hall. He spotted Mel wearing that ratty robe and said, "Well?"

She paused and turned toward him. "God, I feel like a little girl again!"

"Show me."

She hesitated and finally untied the belt and flashed him for a split second. He got a glimpse of her breasts, stomach – and a bare mound between her legs before she closed the robe again and grinned at him.

He went after her and she squealed and ran toward her room. She tried to close the door in his face but he wouldn't have any of it. He banged his way through and grabbed her. She laughed and pretended to fight him off. He pushed her down on the bed, opened her robe and stared at her newly shaved pussy.

"Mr. Rissoli! What do you think you are doing?"

"I'm looking at the most beautiful sight I've ever seen," he responded. "And I'm going to make you come until you can't stand it anymore."

"I'm all tired out! I've come too much!" she protested, but he could tell she didn't mean it. He began suckling on her nipples and she quieted down at once.

"Oh god," she said in a quiet voice. "You're gonna kill me."

"You!?" he said. "I'm the old man here."

She smiled. "You don't seem so old to me, right now. I can't believe that simply shaving would cause such a reaction!"

"Oh yes – and now you're going to make the big bucks, just you wait and see."

She nodded. Neither one spoke for a long while.

Jerry would remember the moment forever. The smooth skin, the scent of her arousal mixed with the fresh clean odor of her body, the new sensitivity of her flesh. He made love to her pussy with his mouth until she begged him to stop. Then he climbed up over her and entered her and she gasped and said, "You're so big!"

He smiled. "That's right, baby. I'm big because of you."

They didn't fuck – they made love, slowly and lovingly. Jerry could almost convince himself that she was his girlfriend, not his whore or his temporary boarder. It was a bittersweet moment.

When they finally separated, exhausted all over again, they lay side by side on the bed and stared at the ceiling.

"I'm going to miss you when you go," he told her.

"I know. But if I don't get a move on, I may never be able to afford to go."

"Yeah." He didn't like to hear that. "So who's the lucky first customer? I mean, for the real thing."

"I think Stu, don't you? He's so eager and said he'd pay two hundred – I still can't believe that."

"Oh, you're worth it, trust me."

"Will you set it up for me?"

He sighed. "Sure." He paused. "How about Tuesday?"

"Sure. That'd work."

"Are you nervous about it?"

"Not right now. But I'm sure I will be Tuesday."

\* \* \*

Wow, she thought. Jerry seemed to be developing a backbone for a minute there. The way he had come in all strong and sexy, it made her swoon a bit. She wondered why – it went against her independent nature. She must be attracted to the strong ones, like Tom. He was forceful too. Nice, but forceful. When they finally started fucking, he did something that sent her over the moon – he grabbed her hair and tugged on it as he fucked the shit out of her. She had come so hard she nearly fell off the bed!

She hadn't realized that shaving would cause such a strong reaction. God, she would've done it ages ago. Maybe Tom would still be with her. Or maybe not – he hadn't seem to have cared. It's a strange fetish. Do men really like it or is Jerry just the exception? She guessed she'd find out Tuesday.

*God, am I really going to fuck a guy? I mean, besides*

*Jerry? She shook her head. Not too late to back out.*

But that other voice in her head piped up: *Yeah, and do what? Idiot. You have to make money, one way or another. And the other way ain't working out too well, is it?*

\* \* \*

Saturday afternoon, they went to the drug store and picked out a new hair color for her. Jerry enjoyed looking at the packages and talking about which might be best for her. She wanted something that would be in the same tone as her light brown hair, but pushed her to go lighter than she thought she should.

"Men really dig blondes," he said. "The lighter the better."

"Oh, so you'd recommend platinum blonde?" She held up the package. It screamed SLUT.

"Uh, no, probably not." *At least, not yet*, he thought. He found another one. "This is what I would recommend."

She took the box. "Medium golden blonde," she read. "Huh. It does look kinda cool."

"Not cool – warm. It will really warm up your looks. I think it's a nice compliment to your current shade."

"Okay. I'll go with your judgment on this."

Jerry offered to pay for it, but Mel insisted. "Oh, no – you've done enough. I have money now, thanks to you."

They returned home and she wanted to color her hair right away. Jerry went into the bathroom with her and helped her with it. He insisted she get naked first, "so she wouldn't stain her clothes," but it was just an excuse and she knew it. Nevertheless, she did what he asked and he spent a delightful hour helping her apply the dye and letting it set, all while she remained naked by the sink.

When she finally jumped in the shower, Jerry couldn't wait to see how it turned out and stayed in the bathroom, watching her wash up behind the semi-transparent curtain.

"Well?" she asked as she stepped out. Steam covered the mirror and she couldn't see for herself.

Jerry gaped at her. She had gone from a mousy but cute cheerleader into a stunning, gorgeous blonde sexpot.

"Gaaaah," he said, his mouth falling open.

She smiled. "I take it that's a good thing?"

He could only nod. She went to the mirror and used the towel to clear a space. She stood there, naked, still dripping, and looked at her wet hair. "It's kinda hard to tell. It will probably look better when it's dry."

"Gaaaah," Jerry said again, nodding.

"Okay, get out, you horndog. Let a girl get ready."

He left at once, his cock pressing against his pants. He waited anxiously in the living room, listening to the hair dryer going and felt like a kid at Christmas. Finally she emerged. He stared. She was even more gorgeous now. Her hair hung in soft waves and although it could use a professional cut, it fairly shimmered around her head, with the highlights catching the sun from the kitchen. His cock wanted her at once.

"Oh. My. God." He approached her slowly, walking around like she was some statue, checking every angle.

"You like?"

"It's amazing. You look great. You could use a little trim, I think."

She nodded. "I thought so too." She dimpled. "You think I'll be able to get customers with this?"

He heart lurched. "Uh, yeah." He tried to get back into his fantasy. "But let's not talk about that today. Today I want you to be mine, okay?"

She shrugged a shoulder. "Okay, as long as you know..."

"Yeah, I know."

He took her back into his bedroom and made love to her again and it was like being with a new girl. Although they had just fucked yesterday – twice – and he still hadn't fully recovered, he felt a renewed sense of excitement and passion that he shared with her. She came twice before he erupted inside her.

"Wow, Jerry, you really spoil me," she told him. "You're ruining me."

"Good. I'm glad."

"When you get a girlfriend, she's going to be the luckiest girl in the world."

"Yeah, I know – you don't have to keep hinting. You're not my girlfriend, okay?"

"Hey, I'm sorry – I meant that as a compliment."

"I know. I'm sorry if I sounded petulant. Sometimes it just slips out."

She hugged him, her naked body next to his. "I know. I'm sorry too."

After dinner, he insisted she sleep with him for the first and last time, telling her it would make his dream come true. She acquiesced, although he could tell she did so reluctantly. He didn't care – just having her in bed with him that night was heaven. He made love to her twice more and she didn't object, but he could sense she was holding a part of herself back from him.

In the morning, he slipped out early and made coffee and went outside to sit at the small table on his patio. He sipped his coffee and thought about calling Stu and offering his girlfriend for him to fuck. That's how he thought of her now, "his girlfriend." He knew it was wrong and he couldn't help it. She had slept with him, made love to him, shaved for him – how could he think of her as a whore?

"This is crazy," he said aloud.

He returned to the kitchen and began making breakfast. Melissa came out a half-hour later, looking sleepy and grabbed a cup of coffee.

"Sleep okay?" he asked.

"Sure, when some guy wasn't humping me," she said in a teasing voice.

He smiled. "That's what you have to put up with from your pimp." He paused. "It wasn't so bad, was it?" He knew he was fishing for compliments and couldn't help it.

She smiled over her coffee cup. "It was nice. Sweet." For a brief moment, Jerry swelled with pride until she dropped the hammer with her follow-up comment. "But it was a one-time deal, right?"

"Uh, right."

She came to him and put a delicate hand on his forearm. "Look, we've talked about this. I've said all along, don't get attached to me. I'm going to go as soon as I can. Don't fall in love with me."

"I know, I know. You're right. It's just hard, you know?"

She tipped her head. "Yeah, I know. You're a sweet man and I hate to lead you on."

*Why can't you just love me?* He asked her in his head, but said nothing.

"I'll call Stu Monday, set it up."

"Okay." She paused. "What's for breakfast?"

And there it was. She had changed the subject, all business now, the girlfriend was gone, not that she had ever existed.

"Scrambled eggs," he said and turned to his work.

Sunday was another bittersweet time for Jerry. They dug in his garden and ate lunch outside, the picture of domestic bliss. In the evening, they made love in her room and afterward she kicked him out, telling him she was tired and wanted to get some sleep. He didn't argue with her or insist. He slunk down the hall feeling blue and tried to get himself into the pimp mindset. It wasn't easy.

Monday, Frank took one look at him and said, "What the hell happened to you? You look like you've aged ten years!"

He gave him a wan smile. "Mel is sucking the life force from me."

"Oh god, you sure have it bad, you bastard! I wish I had a teen-aged girlfriend!"

"No you don't. Especially one as calculating as Mel. Don't get me wrong – she's terrific in bed. Especially now." He briefly described her new hair color and how hot she looked now. "I'm sure she's going to make a great whore."

Frank heard the bitterness in his voice. "Must be tough, huh?"

"Yeah. I mean, I know she's right – she's way too young for me. But she acts old enough, you know?"

"You gotta get her outta there as soon as possible."

"Yeah. Which reminds me: You interested in fucking her?"

"For two hundred? No thanks. I'd love to, but I'll stick with BJs."

"Okay. She's going to start charging fifty for them, but I'll have her do you for thirty, like before."

"Thanks! I appreciate that." He paused. "So, how about tomorrow?"

"I thought you were taking a week off!"

"I did too! But I know this is temporary and I wanted to strike while the iron is hot, if you know what I mean."

"Well, I was going to call Stu for tomorrow. Mel wants to try out her new pussy." He described how she had shaved.

Frank whistled. "Oh, you're killing me, Jerry! Now I've got to find some more money somewhere. Hey, you think she'd do me for a hunnert?"

"I doubt it. But I'll ask her. Maybe a one-time deal or something."

"Hell, you're her pimp, you just tell her!"

"It doesn't work like that."

"Huh. Some pimp you are."

"Let me call Stu, see if he wants tomorrow."

"Wait – what about today? Can she slip me a quick BJ?"

"Uh…" Jerry realized he had subconsciously been saving Mondays for him, but there was no reason why Mel couldn't give Frank a BJ and fuck him later. It was fucking her after she'd fucked someone else that he had a problem with. "Okay, I'll check."

"Check? You really don't know how a pimp works, do you? You're supposed to set up the dates and she's supposed to take care of them. You need to take some pimp lessons. You're more of a wimp than a pimp." He laughed at his own pun.

"Yeah, maybe you're right. It's just that she was going out to get a haircut today. But I think she'll be done by four-thirty. Let me check." He called her and confirmed she'd be back in time. "Okay, you're all set."

Next he called Stu and found the man was eager to try her out.

"So, she's upped the ante?" he asked over the phone, using thinly disguised code.

"Yes, she's ready now."

"Oh my god. Okay, I'm in. And it's still two units? Are you sure we can't work out a deal?"

"No, she insists. And she'll be getting three once people see her new look." He told him about the hair color – let him discover the rest when he was with her.

"Okay, okay, you sold me. God, I can't wait!" He hung up.

Jerry turned to Frank, who had been listening in. "So, her first two customers of the week have been set. Now who else can we get?"

For the next hour, the two men ignored their duties at the school and tossed out names of those who might be discreet enough to enjoy some teen-aged pussy – and who could afford it. That led Frank to come up with an idea that seemed to have a lot of merit.

"My CPA," he said, snapping his fingers. "He's an old horndog. And he knows a lot of rich friends."

"You have an accountant?" Jerry always did his own taxes, as distasteful a job it was.

"I hate doing my taxes. Hate it. I'd rather pay some guy than have to deal with it. And Norman is good. He knows all the angles."

Jerry nodded. "That's good. But he's got to be quiet about this. I mean, I could get into a lot of trouble."

"Hey, you want to find customers or dontcha? This is how we have to do it."

"Yeah, okay, I just worry. I don't look forward to spending a couple years in jail."

"I hear ya. Don't worry. We'll just start with him. Later, I'll ask him to talk to a select few guys – guys he knows he can trust."

"God, this is really happening, isn't it?"

"Yeah, now about that," Frank said. "If I'm the one out there finding customers instead of you, I want a cut."

That took Jerry by surprise. "What?"

"It doesn't have to be money," he continued. "It can be in trade. Say for every two clients I find her, she has to throw me a freebie."

"Ohh, I see." He nodded. "I think we can work

something out. Maybe after every three new clients, huh?"

He made a face. "Give her my first offer and see what she says. She can make a lot of money off of my guys."

"Okay. I'll ask."

Frank shook his head. "Some pimp you are."

"I'd much rather just go back to being a janitor. All this stuff makes me nervous."

## Chapter Ten

Jerry arrived home at four-fifteen and found her relaxing on the couch, wearing ripped jeans and an old Nine Inch Nails T-shirt. Her hair looked great – it had been professionally cut and styled. He whistled.

"You like?" She turned her head this way and that.

"Oh yeah." He frowned. "We're gonna have to get you some new outfits."

She looked down at herself. "What? What's wrong with this?"

"Nothing. You look cute. But you should start wearing sexier clothes. I'm sure you can understand why."

"Oh, sure. I guess."

"Do you own any skirts?"

"Sure. I wear them sometimes. Didn't you see me in them?"

"I can't recall. You mostly wore jeans."

"Yeah, I like 'em." She stood up. "You think I should change?"

"Not for Frank, he won't care. Oh," he added, as if it was nothing, "We have to talk about something first, before Frank gets here." He described how Frank wanted some freebies as an incentive to finding clients.

She nodded. "Oh, I see. So you can't find any on your own? I'm already fucking you."

"I know, I just don't know as many people as Frank does. He travels in the right circles."

"So maybe he should be my pimp, huh?" She said it in a teasing way, but it still stung him.

"Sure, but he'd have to clear it with his wife first." She could not miss the sarcasm in his voice.

"Yeah, well, okay. I get it."

"The point is, he's gonna want to discuss it with you. I think you should hold out for a freebie for every three new clients. He'll push for two."

"What exactly does he mean by a freebie? He likes BJs, right, because he's married and all?"

"No, he wants to fuck you."

"God, men are such pigs."

"Honey, most of your clients will be married. That's the allure here. They can fuck the cute teenager and go home to their bitchy wives whistling a jaunty tune."

"I don't know how men can do that."

"I don't know how women can reject their husbands' advances."

She shrugged. "Yeah, they're both fucked up. Marriage sucks, I guess."

"From what my married friends tell me, that's true."

Jerry heard Frank's car pull up. "He's here. Be strong."

She gave him a half-smile. "You know I am."

Frank knocked and Jerry let him in. Hardly any

words were spoken before Frank took Mel's hand and led her down the hallway. Jerry was curious, not to hear their love-making, but to hear how the conversation went afterward. He crept down the hall and listened by the closed door. He had to endure several minutes of Frank getting his rocks off before he heard the man's zipper go up and he said, "Hey, did Jerry talk to you about my proposal?"

"Yes, just briefly. He said you might have some clients?"

"Yeah. My CPA and his rich friends. You interested?"

"Sure. I guess."

"So here's the deal. For every new client I bring in, I get fifteen percent and a free fuck. Deal?"

That shocked Jerry. It wasn't the deal Frank had proposed to him. Now he wanted a cut of her earnings? That made him wonder if she was still going to offer him his fifty percent cut. He could imagine that Frank's cut – if any – would come out of his end.

"Fifteen percent?" he heard Mel respond. "For every new client? Plus a fuck? No way. How about no money, but I'll throw you a freebie for every three new clients?"

"Oh, no, that sucks. I'm taking the risk here, not Jerry. I know you're slipping him some money. I'm not stupid. Hell, I should be your pimp, not him."

"He's providing the place, plus he rescued me when I was in trouble. I owe him."

"Okay, okay, you owe him. For a little while. And I don't really want to be your pimp, either – I don't want the headache. I'm just saying, I'm doing more for you than he is. So I want a cut. Plus some freebies."

"How about ten percent for each new client – a one-time finder's fee – plus I'll fuck you for every two new clients you bring in?"

There came a long silence. Jerry felt they were close to a deal. Finally, Frank said, "You charge two hundred for a fuck, right?"

"Right. And fifty for a BJ."

"So my cut would only be twenty and five, one time, per client? That's not worth the risk. Forget it."

"What are you offering?"

"Ten percent for each time that client visits you."

"That's unenforceable. You won't know when I'm setting up appointments after the first one."

"Okay, so how about this: Forget the money. For every new client I bring in, you owe me a freebie, either a blow job or a fuck, my choice."

Another silence fell while Mel thought about it. Jerry, standing outside, realized Frank was going to be getting more action that he was. A free fuck for every new client?

In the silence, Frank added, "Including Stu."

"Oh, so you're saying, you want your thirty bucks back."

"Right." A pause. "Well?"

"I'm thinking. I'm just not sure about this. I'd like to talk to Jerry first."

"Hell no, you're the professional. You make your own decisions. He's not even a very good pimp."

"Look, this is all new to me. I know you think I'm some kind of experienced whore and all, but I'm just a kid who's trying to make some money! You know how hard it is to find a job lately?"

"Welcome to the real world, baby. If this is the way you want to earn a living, you've got to play by adult rules. And I promise to take good care of you, bring you lots of rich guys. You'll be living very comfortably."

"All right! All right! A freebie for every new client. One-time fuck or BJ. And here's your thirty dollars back."

Jerry was stunned. He had expected her to be stronger, but Frank manipulated her into become his little whore, just like that.

"Okay, let's seal the deal."

"What?"

"Oh, I know that BJ was for Stu. But I want to see what I'll be getting. Plus, I'll need to see you in order to describe you to my friends."

"You mean, you want me to…"

"That's right. Strip."

Jerry heard the rustle of jeans being unfastened.

"Ohhh, you're very pretty. Oh! And you shave! The men are gonna love you."

"Can I put my clothes on now?"

"No, just a couple minutes more."

Jerry could guess that Frank was putting his hands all over her. He knew the conversation was about over, but he faced another dilemma – he couldn't admit he was eavesdropping. He'd have to hold his anger until he talked to Mel later.

He hurried into the living room and sat down. The door opened a few minutes later and Frank strolled out, a big grin on his face.

"How did it go?" he asked, trying to keep his voice even.

"Great! She gives great head. You're a lucky man."

"Did you make a deal about new clients?"

"Yes, yes we did." He offered no details.

"Well?"

"That's between me and her."

"Come on, she'll tell me in a minute."

"That's between you and her." He checked his watch. "I gotta go. Don't want to keep the wife waiting." He left, leaving Jerry sputtering on the couch.

Melissa came out, looking pensive.

"Well?" he asked, going through the charade of pretending he didn't know the deal already.

"Well, what?"

"Dammit, Mel – what kind of deal did you make?"

"Oh. He's going to be bringing me some new clients and I'm going to fuck him."

"For every one?"

She nodded, her head down. "Yeah. It was the best deal I could make. He wanted money at first."

"He wanted a cut?"

"Yeah. And I'm already paying you – I can't pay him too!"

"You don't have to pay me, Mel. I mean, once you've covered your costs here."

"Oh no! I know you're risking your job plus you're providing the house. No, I insist on paying you."

"Okay." He was pleased. It seemed to assuage his unrequited love. If he couldn't have Mel, he could at least have some money. "Fifty percent, right? And you just got thirty, right?"

She grimaced. "Uh, no. That was a freebie for Stu."

"Oh."

"And about that. The fifty percent, I mean. I'd like to cut that down to thirty." She hurried on when she saw his startled expression. "That way, I can move out sooner, Jerry. Plus, you're getting freebies right and left."

She was right, but it still seemed wrong, somehow. "Some pimps get seventy percent and give their girls thirty. Or less." He wasn't sure if that was true, but he'd seen it in movies.

"Hey, I'll pay you the fifty if you want. But that will mean I'll be here, with guys, driving you crazy, for many more weeks. Maybe longer. Is that what you want?"

Jerry was torn. He did want to have her around to fuck whenever he wanted. But at what cost! To hear her in the next room, crying out her passion while some stranger fucked her! He shuddered.

"Okay. Thirty percent. And you move out as soon as you can."

She came to him and gave him a brief hug, which he did not return. "Don't worry, I'll be out as soon as Frank comes through for me. I've already been looking for places."

"Really? You find anything interesting?"

"Yes. There are some nice studio apartments I could get for about seven-fifty. I think I could afford that. I mean, if things work out."

"Oh, I think you'll be making a lot more money

than you imagine – as long as you don't give it away free too much."

She frowned. "I know. But it seemed like the best deal I could make. I wanted to talk it over with you first, but Frank wanted an answer right away."

"Okay. I understand. Besides, if he becomes too much of a pest, you can always threaten to tell his wife."

"Oh yeah, that'd go over great. No, I think I need to keep on Frank's good side, especially if he's going to be bringing in all my new clients."

Inwardly, Jerry winced. And what was he doing? He wracked his brain to think of people he knew and realized he didn't know very many. Oh, he had casual friends, but no one he'd approach to offer them a whore. For the first time, he realized he was out of his depth.

"Come on," he said, abruptly changing the subject. "I want my freebie."

"Right now?" she whined.

"Yes, right now. It's Monday, you know."

"Okay, okay." She followed him to his room.

The fucking was perfunctory and not entirely satisfying. He came, of course, but he suspected she was faking her orgasm. He did not ask. He didn't want to know.

Both Jerry and Melissa were antsy as five o'clock approached Tuesday. He was home forty-five minutes before the appointment, giving him time to go over the ground rules – "Get the money up front and scream if you get into trouble" – and talk about her feelings now that she was going to fuck a stranger for the first time.

"Are you afraid?"

"Yeah, sort of. I mean, I've been fucking you regular, so I know what to expect, but it's different, you know?" She had on a knee-length tan skirt and white blouse and looked like she was heading off to a formal date. But her legs looked great and Jerry knew Stu would be appreciative.

"I know. But at least you know Stu, sort of."

"Yeah. He's nice. He's eager as a puppy in many ways. I just wonder how he'll behave once I'm in bed with him."

"Make sure he wears a condom. No exceptions." Jerry made a mental note to go buy more.

"I will. But what if he doesn't want to? I'm not big enough to fight him off."

"Just scream, like I told you, and I'll come running." He glanced over at the fireplace and spotted the poker there. He pictured himself howling like a banshee, brandishing the poker overhead as he crashed into the room. "Wear a condom, you asshole!" he'd shout. The very idea made him laugh at himself.

"Yeah, but it makes me nervous to think about being in my own place."

Jerry had no response to that for a moment. Then: "Maybe you should hook up with an escort service. They'd protect you."

She made a face. "I'm still thinking about that."

They heard a car pull up outside and Jerry went to the window to peek out. "It's Stu. He's a little early."

"I told you: He's like a puppy."

"Okay. Get ready."

"God."

The doorbell rang. Jerry opened it and stepped back. Stu nodded in his direction. "Hi, Jerry." He turned at once to see Mel standing there in her skirt, looking like a schoolgirl. "Oh my god, you look gorgeous, Jami. Did you dress up for me?"

She nodded, too afraid to speak.

Jerry jumped in. "You know the price and all, Stu?"

"Yeah." His eyes never left Melissa. They seemed to eat her up.

"Okay, then. I'll let you two guys take care of business. I'm going to step out for a bit."

Mel looked up in shock for a second before getting herself under control. "You're leaving?"

"Just for a few minutes. To give you guys a little privacy. Don't worry, I'll be back."

"Uh, okay."

"Yeah, that's a good idea, Jerry. Give us some privacy," Stu said and stepped forward to take both of her hands into his. "You really are gorgeous, you know that?"

"Aw, thanks, Sam. You're sweet."

It was the same thing she had said to Jerry, many times. He stepped to the door. "I'll be back in a bit," he said and closed it behind him. He hadn't intended to leave, but he had suddenly been overwhelmed with a desire not to hear their love-making. He was familiar with the sounds she made in bed and didn't think he could handle hearing them with another man.

What an idiot he had been, thinking she was falling for him, just a little bit. Despite all the evidence to the contrary, Jerry still believed she might wind up as his girlfriend. How naïve could he be? He was like those crazed fans who drive across the country to find their "soulmate" – some actress who he had only see on TV – and expect to marry her. Being arrested never seemed to stop those nuts. Was he the same way? Not far from it, he told himself.

He didn't want to leave Mel alone too long – she might actually need his help. So he walked quickly around the block and re-entered his home. He could hear them at once. The thump of the bed, the passionate cries from Mel, the rising crescendo of Stu's voice as he neared his climax. He was really fucking her brains out! He stood frozen in the foyer and listened until Stu reached his peak and Mel cried out with an orgasm, either real or faked, he couldn't tell. Silence fell and he moved to the couch to sit down. He found himself breathing heavily and he struggled to calm down. His emotions were causing his body to jerk as if he'd been tasered.

The door opened and Stu came out, grinning. "My, that's a fine piece of ass you've got there, Jerry."

Jerry put on a plastic smile and nodded. "Yes, she is. Worth every penny." It hurt his face to get the words out without screaming.

"Got that right. Hey, I might know of someone who would like a taste. You okay with that?"

"Sure, just call me with a name first. We don't want this to spread around too much, you know?

And keep it to yourself. Don't share it with Frank, even."

"Really? God, you are paranoid."

"Hey, this is illegal, you know."

"I know. But she needs customers, from what I've been told."

"Sure."

He left a short time later and Jerry breathed a sigh of relief. Mel came out and went immediately into the bathroom. He heard the shower go on. He shook his head. Poor girl, she must be traumatized.

When she came out, a half-hour later, her calm demeanor surprised Jerry. She had on her robe and her hair wrapped up in a towel. She came up to him and gave him a peck on the cheek and with one hand slipped him a few bills. He looked down to see three twenties there. His cut.

"How did it go?"

"It went fine. I was nervous for nothing. He was a perfect gentleman."

"Did you come?" The words slipped out before he could stop them. But he wanted to know.

She paused and turned fully toward him. "Why do you ask?"

"Well, uh… I heard you. Either you were being a great actress, like I had suggested, or…"

Mel pursed her lips as if debating whether to answer him. "I'm not sure you need to know that."

"Yes, I do," he said. "I mean, as your pimp, I might want to critique your technique." His argument was so lame as to be laughable but neither one laughed.

"Would you be jealous if I told you the truth?"

At that moment, Jerry knew the truth. He tried to maintain his composure. "I think you just told me. And I'm glad for you. I'm glad that he, uh, made you feel good."

"Really?"

"Yeah. I know you were nervous and all. You wondered if you were doing the right thing or if he'd get violent or something. That's why you wanted me around. But you saw that he was very nice to you, very appreciative of the intimacy. And I'm actually glad it all worked out, even though I admit to a bit of jealousy."

"Well, I expected that. I mean, it's one thing for me to give some guy a BJ in your home, but quite another… well, you know."

He nodded. "Emotionally, it's a bit tough. But you've always been straight with me, so I've got my mind right, as they say. Besides, part of me was a little turned on by all that."

Her eyes widened. "Really?"

"Really. I can't explain it. But the idea that you were in there fucking a guy… well, I felt both jealous and turned on. Does that make sense?"

"I don't know. I guess that's better than just being jealous."

He nodded. "Yeah."

# Chapter Eleven

Frank and Stu came through and business began to pick up after that first week. On Monday, Melissa – who had seemed to become Jami, the whore, before his eyes – serviced Norman, the CPA. He was followed by Frank the very next day, getting his freebie. Wednesday, a client recommended by Frank named Charlie came by. He was a balding, rotund lawyer and told her if he liked what he saw, he'd recommend her to his friends. He clearly did. Thursday one of those clients, another lawyer named James, stopped by. Friday, she fucked Frank again.

It turned out, Mel didn't have to worry much about Frank and his freebies. Many of the new clients were recommending others, bypassing Frank entirely. His freebies started out strong, but by the end of August, he was lucky to get one a week. Plus, Frank's wife was becoming suspicious, he admitted to Jerry, and was wondering why he was coming home so late from work every day. The excuse that he was "just stopping by Jerry's for a beer" had worn thin.

Stu remained her favorite client those first few weeks, although he could only afford her once every two weeks or so. Coming on a strong second was James, the tall, thin lawyer with graying hair. He always made her come at least twice, and Jerry could tell she wasn't faking it. Plus, he was making suggestions to her on how she might make more money. She shared a few of his ideas with Jerry, who had trouble hiding his shock.

"James says I can charge five hundred an hour if I'm willing to do some things," she told him over dinner one night.

"Such as?"

"Like, uh, spankings and such." She caught Jerry's startled expression and hurried on. "Men like to spank women, he says. It's a big turn-on. Something to do with how helpless men feel today, you know, with all the women's lib stuff."

"Uh huh."

"He says if I buy a riding crop and let men whip me a few times before I fuck them, I could charge five hundred instead of two."

"Really?" He did the math in his head. He'd get one-fifty. That was real money. "That sounds painful."

"Yeah, but I'd have a safe word, he says. And if the clients violated it, they'd never get to come back. That way, I'd be protected."

"Huh. Are you going to do it?"

"I'm thinking about it. I mean, five hundred! That's a lot of money."

"What other ideas has he been suggesting?"

"Well, uh…" She seemed reluctant to say. Jerry just waited her out. "He said some guys like to tie up a girl first."

"What? That sounds dangerous!"

"I know! I'm not too keen on that idea. But I'd be making the big bucks if I did."

"You could also wind up dead."

"Not if I only do it here, while you're here."

"You said yourself you want to move out as quickly as possible. So let's say you let a client do that to you and a month later, you move into your own place and he calls you for a date. You think he's going to want to skip that new game you've been playing? Not only that, but once he knows you're in your own place and have no one to come rescue you, he could go much further than you want him to."

"Really? God, I hadn't thought of it that way."

"You need some burly black guy with a shaved head around, just for those occasions. Scare the shit out of those white businessmen if they get out of line."

She laughed. "Yeah, maybe I do."

"That gets us back to signing with an escort agency. You can't do this alone. You need support."

"I'm beginning to realize that. You've been great, you know. I wish you could be my pimp – I mean, going forward."

"I know. But I'm not exactly intimidating. Plus, I don't want to go to jail."

"Okay. But how about the, uh, spanking thing. That seems harmless enough, doesn't it?"

"Same thing. Sure, while I'm here. But if you go down that road and you're in your own place, maybe he won't be satisfied with a riding crop. Maybe he'll bring his own cane or something, tear up your bottom. Some men are really into hurting whores."

"God, I must sound really naïve."

"Yeah, you do."

"Okay, I'll think about it. But I still want to make more money, if I can."

"I know. Just be careful, that's all. I don't want to read about you in the papers."

The days became a blur for Jerry as September opened and the first day of school neared. Jami was quickly becoming a popular whore. Men of all ages came by, often two per day, and the money began to pile up. Mel kept thrusting wads of cash at him and he wondered where she was keeping all of hers. He asked her about it one Friday afternoon after her last customer left.

"Oh, uh, I have it stashed away somewhere."

"It's not safe, Mel. You need to have a bank account."

"How am I going to explain it? I mean, I know banks get suspicious. If I walk in there with three thousand dollars a week?"

"That much?" He did the math in his head and realized she was earning that much. He had made almost fifteen hundred himself.

"Yeah."

"We need to figure out a laundering scheme." It made Jerry realize just how much he was out of his depth on this. "Why don't you ask Norman?"

"Oh! Right! I should've thought of that. He's coming by Monday."

"Uh, good." Jami – it was becoming harder to think of her as Melissa now – was so popular, she hardly had time for him anymore. She offered him blow jobs whenever he wanted, but often claimed she was "too sore" to fuck him, which is what he really wanted. Her position in his home was becoming untenable. The neighbors had to be wondering why so many men were stopping by.

She caught his expression. "I know," she said.

"What?" he pretended innocence.

"It's time. I mean, I need to find my own place."

"Well…"

"I'm sorry – I know I should have moved already. It's just been so safe, here with you."

"I'm hardly intimidating. I mean, to your, uh, customers."

"Just having you here makes me feel safe. That's what has kept me from moving yet. But I know it's time." She paused. "Uh, that's why I …" she trailed off.

"What?"

"Maybe I feel insecure. About the money and all. Hell, I've probably got close to eight grand saved and I'm still nervous – isn't that crazy? Anyway, I decided to try something new. For more money." She looked away.

"What? What did you agree to?"

Her voice dropped in volume. "Uh, James is coming by tomorrow."

"James? Tomorrow?" It had been an unspoken agreement between them than weekends were for him. Or for resting. Either way, she had not made any appointments for Saturday before. "What gives?"

"He's, uh, gonna pay me five hundred. And he's gonna do some stuff."

"Oh, you mean like… spanking?"

She nodded.

"And you're going to let him?"

"He said he'd show me how it's done. He'd take it easy on me. Plus, you'll be here. I mean, won't you?"

"I thought we talked about this. Sure, I might be here, although it will be hard for me to sit idly by and listen to you get whipped. But even if I did and everything went well, what happens when you get your own place? Who's gonna watch out for you then?"

"Maybe you could come by or something," she said it as a joke, but he knew she was tossing out the idea to gauge his reaction.

"No way," he told her. "You know how I feel about you. I can't stand around and listen to your… abuse."

"But will you tomorrow? Just for this first time? I promise I won't ask you to do it again."

Jerry considered it. There was really no other choice. He wasn't going to abandon her, like everyone else had in her young life. "Okay."

"Oh, thank you! And you've earned a reward!" She grabbed his hand and tugged him to his feet.

He pretended to resist. "Are you sure? I don't want a pity fuck."

She made a face. "It's not like that. I'm going to be gone soon and I'll miss you. And I know you'll miss me. So let's have fun while we can, okay?"

He smiled. "Well, since you put it that way…"

He made love to her and enjoyed the sensations of her young pussy clutching at him. He managed to hold off long enough to watch her climax before he reached his own release. She sighed and snuggled down into his arms. He lay there and thought about what might have been.

Saturday, Jami was nervous. "I'm not sure I want to do this," she told him over breakfast.

"What time is he coming by?"

"Eleven."

Jerry checked his watch. "It's almost ten now. Not too late to change your mind. Call him and cancel."

"No!" She shook her head. "He's gonna pay me five hundred! For one hour! Can you believe it?"

"Yeah, but he's going to whip your bottom and god knows what else. Did you agree on the ground rules, at least?"

"That's what we're going to work through. He promised not to scare me or hurt me or anything. He said it will make the sex better."

"Yeah, for him, maybe."

"Yeah."

"Just how many of these new type of clients do you plan to take on before you move out?"

"I don't know. I'm just doing this as an experiment, you know. I may run screaming from the room and that will be that."

"Okay. I hope you know what you are doing."

She nodded and began clearing the dishes. "Well, I'd better get ready."

"Yeah."

Jerry felt strange, watching Melissa lose herself to Jami, and felt helpless to bring her back to earth. *It's your funeral*, he thought. She went into the bathroom and closed the door. He thought about James and his fetish. Spanking, huh? He had to admit, it did excite him too. He wasn't sure why. But the idea of spanking that cute butt with his bare hand made him hard.

Jerry had a sudden inspiration. He waited until he heard the shower turn on and went to the door. His hand wrapped around the knob and he turned it and noted it gave. He opened the door a crack and heard Jami in the shower, humming to herself as she showered. He quickly stepped in and stripped off his clothes. He pulled aside the curtain to see Jami with shaving cream all over her pussy, one leg up on the edge of the tub. She startled when she saw him and shook her head.

"You scared me!"

"I thought I'd join you."

"Did I say you could?"

"I'm your pimp. At least for now. You have to do what I say."

She smiled. "I do, do I?"

"Yes, you do. Or I'll have to spank you."

Her eyes went wide and she raised her eyebrows. He stepped in and got wet under the spray before squatting down directly in front of her lathered pussy and nodding to her. "Go ahead. I want to watch."

"You're getting a little kinky, huh?"

"Uh huh."

She began to shave. "Does that turn you on, watching me?"

"Yes." Her bare pussy slowly began to emerge. His eyes were riveted on her.

"And thinking about spanking me? Does that do it as well?"

He nodded. "Maybe I should've volunteered to be your first."

She laughed. "You tried to talk me out of it!"

"I know, but now that you're going to do it, I've had a chance to rethink it."

"Ohhh. So maybe you're just as bad as James."

"I don't know. I don't know how far James is going to go."

"Yeah, I don't either. I'm still a little nervous about that."

She finished shaving and she straightened up but she did not rinse off, giving Jerry a few more seconds to stare at her freshly bare pussy. When he finally glanced up, she said, "Seen enough?"

"Never." He stood and took her into his arms. She came eagerly, rubbing her wet body up against his. He reached behind her and gave her bottom a playful slap. "How's that feel?"

"Not bad," she breathed.

He struck her again on the other cheek.

"But you can't," she said.

He stopped and pulled back. "What?"

"James wants my bottom to be unmarked. He insisted."

"Ohhh." Of course, Jerry thought. He wants to mark it himself. "Okay."

He pulled back and began to wash up. She washed up as well and when they were done, they both stepped out onto the mat side by side.

"Turn around."

She did and he noted the slightly pink marks he had left were already fading. "You'll be fine. Can't tell a thing."

She craned her neck over her shoulder. "I hope not! I don't want to ruin things."

"I'm sure he'll love you. I just hope you'll be okay."

"I think I will. James seems harmless enough."

When Jami came out of her bedroom at quarter to eleven, she wore a yellow sundress. It was obvious she wasn't wearing a bra. He whistled from the couch. "You look great. I don't think I've seen that dress before."

"James bought it for me. He insisted I wear it."

"Let me guess – he said, 'Wear this dress and nothing else,' right?"

She nodded. "How did you know?"

"I think I'm starting to understand James a little better. He likes to control things."

"Yes."

"How do you feel about that?"

"I'm not sure yet."

"Well, you should have a safe word, okay? Something to make him stop. Because you can't rely on me, you know."

"No?"

"No. I mean, I'd come running in if I thought you were being hurt, but it will be hard to tell the difference between excited cries and real pain, you know?"

She nodded. "I hadn't thought of it that way. Okay."

He smiled. "Twirl around for me."

She did so and the lightweight material swirled up around her knees.

"Do it again. Spin faster."

"Jerry!"

"Come on, just once more."

She did and her skirt swirled up almost to the vee of her legs. For a split second, Jerry thought he caught a glimpse of her bare pussy. She staggered sideways and caught herself on the arm of the couch. "Okay! Enough. I'm getting dizzy."

"It was sooo sexy," he told her. "Now, stand still. Turn around and show me your butt."

"Jerry!"

"Come on, I'm just making sure your little pink marks have faded."

"So you did leave marks!"

"Barely. Come on, show me."

She turned and lifted her skirt and Jerry was a little disappointed to see they had vanished.

"Well?"

"You're okay. Your bottom is pristine, ready for your whipping." He paused. "What will he be using on you? Did you go over that?"

"Kinda. He said he wanted to bring a few toys, as he called them. He wanted me to experiment, just a little."

"Be careful. If he brings out a cane, run."

"A cane? Why, does that hurt?"

"You are naïve. A cane hurts like a son-of-a-bitch.

Haven't you seen pictures on the Internet?"

"Uh, no – it's not the kind of thing I look for."

Jerry felt a little embarrassed because it was obvious he had.

The doorbell rang, freezing them both. Jerry tipped his head. "I think you ought to answer it."

She nodded and took a deep breath. She opened the door and greeted the man standing there. "Hi, James."

James was tall and he carried himself like he was made of money, which he probably was. He had on tailored gray suit and red power tie, which struck Jerry as odd for a Saturday. Didn't the guy ever relax? From the gray in his hair, Jerry estimated his age was about fifty. His square head seemed to swivel as he took in the room and finally, Jerry. He gave a curt nod. He turned back to Jami.

"Are you ready, my dear?" At his side, he carried a soft leather briefcase. Jerry noted how Jami's eyes seemed to lock onto it.

"Uh, we need to discuss a safe word, first," she said, glancing over at Jerry.

James smiled. "Of course. Let's go into your room for that." Without another look at Jerry, he took Jami's hand and led her down the hall. Jerry heard the lock click loudly. He waited a few minutes, then got up and tip-toed toward the door.

\* \* \*

Inside, Melissa stood nervously while James took off his suitcoat and hung it up. He had on a gray vest underneath. He hefted the briefcase onto the bed and sat down next to it. He patted the space next to him.

"Sit down, my dear."

She did, feeling the butterflies in her stomach.

"So you want a safe word, hmm?"

"Yes."

"For this session, I'd prefer to be called 'sir.' Do you mind?"

"No, I mean, no, sir."

"Good. If you are to do this successfully, you must play the part. It's best if you really feel it, deep in here," he said, his hand patting her stomach through the dress. "But for now, you can just play along, okay?"

She nodded.

"You didn't say, 'yes, sir.' That's worthy of punishment."

Her heart began to beat faster. "Yes, sir."

"Now, to your safe word." He gave her a slow smile. "I'm thinking a phrase will be better, so there's no misunderstanding. Does that sound good?"

"Yes, sir."

"Okay. If things get too intense, I want you to shout out, 'This slut is unworthy!' Can you remember that?"

"Yes, sir, but—"

"I know, it might seem an odd phrase to you, but it will be true, you see. If you can't take it, you *will* be unworthy. It's not only a safe word, but it also brings up a sense of shame that you failed to endure your punishment like a good girl."

"I thought we were just going to experiment a little," she said timidly.

"Oh, we are. I'm just trying to help you understand the protocol surrounding this type of sexual stimulation. That is, if you want to earn the big bucks."

"I'm … I'm not entirely sure yet. That's what I'm hoping to learn from this." She added quickly, "Sir."

"Of course." He turned to his briefcase. "Now, I'm sure you'd like to know what I brought. Frankly, I probably brought more than we'll need in one hour. But I wanted to give you a little taste of each item." He opened the flap. "First, we have the good ol' riding crop." He pulled it out.

Melissa could see it was about sixteen inches long, made of some sort of stiff material, with a leather flap at one end. She swallowed.

"This is my smallest model. I also have one eighteen inches and one twenty-two inches." He waved it in the air. "Would you like to see how it works?"

"I'm not sure I do."

"What did you want to charge me for this session? Was it two hundred?"

"You said five!"

"Right. So let me ask you again: Would you like to see how it works?"

"Uh, yes. Yes, sir."

"Good. Please stand up."

Mel did, her nerves jangling. He turned her away from him and gave her a quick slap through her dress with the crop. She hardly felt it.

"There, that wasn't so bad, was it?"

"No, sir."

"Good. See, it's often scarier than you think it is." He put the crop aside and pulled out another whip.

Mel turned to look. It seemed to be a horrific object, made of several strands of leather, attached to a thick handle.

"This, my dear, is a cat o'nine tails. I brought my softest one, made of suede. Here, feel it."

She did and noted it did feel rather soft. She nodded.

"Let's try it out as well, shall we?"

She nodded and turned away. He gave her a quick slap on her bottom with it. Again, it tingled more than it hurt. She smiled. "That's not bad either. Uh, sir."

"See? It's really more about stimulation than punishment, although your clients will want to pretend to be whipping you to get their own blood boiling. If you can take a few swats with objects such as these, you can just about name your price."

"Really?"

"Oh yes. You could easily earn two or three thousand dollars in a single night."

"Gosh."

"I have a couple more things. Sad to say, my cane wouldn't fit in this briefcase. But I did bring a leather paddle. See?"

The object was a thick, flat leather strap about fifteen inches long, of which about one-third was handle. The strap part was about three inches wide and surprisingly thick.

"This is made from the finest English saddle leather," James told her, caressing the strap. "It's my favorite. You'll see why. May I?" He held it up.

Mel shook a little as she turned sideways to him. She didn't want to feel that on her bottom! It looked lethal. He gave her a slap with it. She jumped, but more out of fear than pain.

"How was that?"

"Uh, it was okay."

"See, these things don't hurt too much. But your clients will want to leave some red marks – it's all part of the game. Those marks usually fade away within a day."

"Really?"

"Oh yes." He pulled another object out of his briefcase. It was similar to the riding crop, but smaller, about a foot long, ending in a leather taper instead of a flap.

"This is also very popular. Do you know what it's used for?"

"Uh, my bottom?" she asked.

James smiled. "No, my dear. This is a pussy whip." He whipped it in the air a few times.

"Oh my god! I'm not letting you come near me with that!"

"You'd be surprised. It can make a girl climax so powerfully, she comes to beg for it."

"I don't know..."

"Well, don't make judgments until you've tried it." He put it down on the bed and Jami repressed a little shiver.

"Now, I also have one more thing that you might experience during your adventures in this realm." He stood up and unbuckled his belt. It was a thick, well-worn belt with rounded edges. He folded it over and showed it to her.

"See how old and smooth this is? I had this made

from an old schoolmaster's belt at a Scottish boarding school. I had it cut down a bit, but otherwise, it's just like it was back when it was used, in the thirties and forties."

He made her touch it. She did and noted how smooth it felt, yet it was so thick! It made her stomach flutter anew. "You… you hit girls with this?"

"This one was used on boys, but yes. Now I use it exclusively for girls. And women. You'd be surprised at how it intensifies the sexual experience."

*For whom?* she thought but did not say.

"Now," he said, suddenly all business. "Shall we get started?"

Melissa hesitated. Did she really want to do this? "I don't know."

"You said you wanted to see what was involved in making a lot of money. This is it."

Maybe she was just being a baby, she thought. Nothing he tried out on her hurt. She should at least try it. "Okay."

"Okay, what?"

"Okay, sir."

"Better. Now, let's get this dress off, shall we?"

She stood still while he bent down and grabbed the hem. Pulling it up, he lifted it over her head and off, tossing it to the side. Mel was completely naked now. He nodded his approval.

"Good. I see you obeyed my instructions. You've avoided additional punishment."

She didn't like the sound of that.

"Please bend over the edge of the bed, feet on the floor."

She did, her butt up and exposed. She tried not to shake.

"I'm going to let you decide what to start with first," he told her.

"Uh… the riding crop." It seemed the most harmless of the lot.

"Good choice. That's like a fine clear wine to drink before dinner – and the belt would be the cabernet. But let's get you into the right frame of mind, shall we? I want you to say, 'Sir, I deserve to be whipped with the riding crop.' See the difference?"

"Uh, yeah. I mean, yes, sir, I guess." She paused and when he said nothing, she went on, "Uh, I deserve to be whipped with the riding crop, sir."

"Good. Excellent." He reared back and without any preamble, struck her right butt-cheek hard with the crop.

Mel screamed and jumped up, her hands behind her. "Ow! Ow!"

Almost immediately, she heard Jerry at the door, knocking. "You okay in there?"

James shook his head sadly, as if painfully disappointed. "I guess you don't want to earn a lot of money."

"I'm okay," she shouted, determined to finish what she had started. James had promised her five hundred for the hour and by god, she was going to earn it!

"Are you sure? It doesn't sound like it."

"Tell him you have a safe word and that I promised to stop when you have had enough," James said quietly.

Mel went to the door and opened it a crack. Jerry's eyes widened when he saw she was naked. "You sure about this?"

"Yes, I'm sure," she told him. "I have a safe word and James will honor it. So please don't come in again unless I call your name, okay?"

"Okay, if you say so."

She closed the door and turned toward James. "Sorry about that."

He shrugged. "He's just being protective of his live-in lover."

"It's not like that… I mean…"

"I understand. He's clearly in love with you but you're not with him. All the more reason to get your own place, right?"

She nodded. She turned around to see the red triangle on her pale bottom. "You really left a mark!"

"It will fade by tomorrow. Now, shall we continue?" He looked at his watch and added, "You really do owe me a few more minutes with all these delays."

"Uh, okay." She tried to get back into the mood. "Sir."

He smiled. "Good! See? You're a quick learner. But it's important to stay in character. You need to think of yourself as a submissive woman, who deserves to be punished. You've done something very wrong, see, and you must atone."

She nodded. "Okay. Just go a little easy on me, okay?"

James tipped his head. "I'm just trying to prepare you for others, if you want to try it out."

"I see."

He led her back to the bed and pressed her down as before. "I have to even out the marks, then we'll move on, okay?"

"Uh, okay. I mean, sir."

"Say, 'I've been bad and I need to be punished.' That might help you get into character."

"I've been bad and I need to be punished... sir."

"Good! Excellent!"

Whack! The crop fell on her other bottom cheek and this time, Melissa merely jerked and grunted.

James immediately put his hand on her bottom and caressed it. "Oh, that was much better! See, you can do this."

"Okay."

"Let's do two more quickly and we'll move on."

Before she could say anything, he struck her right and left. Mel grunted and bit her lip, but she did not cry out or jump up. He bent down and kissed the small of her back, his fingers barely touching the marks on her bottom. She shivered and realized she was getting wet. It embarrassed her that she could react that way.

"Now," James continued, straightening up. "Let's try the suede cat o'nine tails next, shall we?"

She nodded and braced herself. When he struck her, it didn't hurt as much as the crop, which surprised her. The leather spread out over her entire ass and each strand was soft. There was only a brief bolt of pain, followed by a heating of her loins.

"Ohhh," she moaned.

"Yes, this is much better," James said and proceeded to whip her from the left for about thirty seconds before switching to the right.

Melissa quickly found the pain racheted up as long as he was striking her, but when he stopped, even for the few seconds it took to change sides, her pussy grew so hot she felt she was gushing fluids. She began to jerk her hips to rub her clit against the covers. She could almost come!

He stopped and stepped in to grab her hips, preventing her from climaxing.

"Ohhh," she protested.

"No, no, you don't get to come until I say so. It's part of the game."

"God."

"How was that?"

"It was… it was incredible."

"Oh, I think you've found your new favorite toy."

She peered over her shoulder to see her entire bottom covered in faint red marks left by the cat o'nine tails, in sharp contrast to the bright red marks left by the crop.

"Now, let's try the leather paddle."

Mel wasn't sure she was ready for something like that. "Can't we do the belt first?"

"No," he said simply. "We can't."

Whack! She jerked and screamed. This did not feel good at all! She tried to rise but he held her down with his free hand and struck her again.

"Ow! Ow!" She tried to remember her safe phrase. "Uh, this slut…"

Whack! Whack!

"This slut is unworthy!"

James stopped at once and began to rub his hand

lightly over her sore bottom.

"Ow, that one really hurt."

"I know. It can be a formidable punishment. This one is usually reserved for very bad girls."

She shivered and promised herself she'd never be that bad.

"I think I've had enough," she said.

"Don't you mean, 'I think I've had enough, *sir*?'"

"Uh, yeah, that's what I meant."

"Well, so far, you've earned about two-fifty. And I haven't even fucked you yet. Wouldn't you like to earn the whole five hundred?"

"What else do I have to do? Can't you just fuck me now?"

"No, I have to use the belt. Just four strokes. And the pussy whip. Four strokes. Then I'll fuck you. If you can do all that, you will have earned all of the money."

She wasn't sure about the pussy whip. But he had said she should try it first. "Can you go easy on me?"

"Yes, yes I can," he said.

"All right." She settled down and gripped the bed covers with both hands and waited. She heard the jingle of the buckle as he picked up the belt and glanced back to make sure it was safely out of the way. James had doubled over the soft belt and was making a few experimental swipes in the air. It didn't appear he was going to hit her too hard so she settled back into place and waited.

The blows came quickly, one after the other – hard, across both cheeks. She was startled, then shocked. The pain rocketed up her spine to her head and before she could say, "OW!" and give her safe word, it was over.

"This slut is unworthy!" she shouted anyway into the now-quiet room.

"You are doing great, Jami. I'm very pleased."

She stood and noticed his erection tenting his pants. She looked over her shoulder at her bright red bottom. It send waves of heat into her loins.

"Now, for the pussy whip, I'll only do it lightly, so you can see what I'm talking about."

"I'm not sure, James. I mean, sir. It looks like it will really hurt."

"That's just your fear talking. You should at least know how exquisite it can be. That is, if you want to make good money." The way he said it sounded like a threat.

"Well, just go easy, okay?"

"Okay, what?"

"Okay, sir."

"Please get on your back."

She did and winced with pain when her sore bottom rubbed against the sheets.

"Lift your legs up and apart."

It made her feel very exposed, but it did help ease the pain of her bottom. She looked up at him from between her legs, her breathing coming hard now, her heart pounding. James took the pussy whip and flicked it lightly against her mound, missing her clit by a fraction of an inch. She had expected a bolt of pain, but instead, it tingled as the heat radiated outward. She relaxed a little.

"See? It's not so bad."

"No, not as long as you do it like that."

The next blow hit the other side of her clit and she jerked and heat increased. Her pussy was dripping wet. It made her feel really slutty to be lying there, watching herself get whipped. The third blow was also gentle and it struck her directly on her clit, but with the fat end of the tapered leather. She gasped in shock for it made her entire body feel as if she had been electrocuted. She started to close her legs but James put his hands in the way.

"Only one more now and then we're done. Can you do one more for me, sweetheart?"

She nodded, unable to speak. What was happening to her?

The last blow came down hard, striking her clit with the tip of the whip and she screamed and arched her back. She wasn't sure if she was about to die or about to come, it was that powerful.

She looked up at him to see he was unfastening his pants. His cock was veiny and hard. He plunged into her all at once and the feeling was incredible. She forgot herself for a moment and was transported into a pleasure/pain loop that made her swoon.

She gasped with sudden realization. "I'm ... You have to wear a condom!"

But it was too late. Her pussy was so wet, he slipped right in and although she struggled, he was far bigger and stronger than she was. He easily held her down while he pumped away, bringing her to an orgasm within seconds. It was almost painful, due to the whipping of her pussy. Within a minute, he came and she felt his cock throb deep inside her.

He pulled out and got up. She lay there a moment before her wits returned. Angrily, she rolled to her feet. "You... you bastard! You're supposed to wear a condom!"

Without a word, James zipped himself up, pulled out his wallet and counted out five one-hundred dollar bills. He tossed them on the bed next to her and began gathering up his equipment.

She stared at the money. Five hundred! It was more than she had ever earned before. Her anger began to leach away. She grabbed it and stood up, found her dress and slipped it on over her head.

"You were supposed to wear a condom."

James smiled at her, ignoring her resentment. He slipped on his suit coat. "Thank you, my dear. You were worth every penny. If you'd like to explore this more, once you get over your shock, please give me a call." He dropped his business card on the bed. "I have many friends who would pay this much or more for an evening with you."

"But... how can I trust you? Or any of your friends?"

"My friends are quite trustworthy. And none of them have any diseases. But that's what you must expect when you make the big bucks. Rich men don't like condoms. Let me know what you decide." He opened the door and left, leaving her standing there, butt and pussy throbbing, his seed running down one thigh, her mind in turmoil.

# Chapter Twelve

Jerry watched Jami come out of the bedroom and waited for her to talk to him. Like before, she went immediately into the bathroom and he resisted the urge to follow her in. Let her come to him of her own accord. It had shocked him to hear her cries of pain. He had given the lawyer a dirty look but not much else and felt guilty about it. What was going on here? Did she like that sort of thing?

Jerry wasn't naïve, he knew some girls got off on the pain/pleasure dichotomy. He had seen web sites devoted to such things. They had seemed to be designed for the men, not the women. If Jami wanted to go down that road, he would have to insist she move out right away. He couldn't have his neighbors hear a girl screaming in here!

The shower went on and he knew it would be at least a half-hour. He went and grabbed a beer, although it was only a few minutes after noon. He needed a drink. He felt like Melissa was moving further and further away from him and all that remained was this whore Jami. As much as he liked fucking her, he found the baggage that came along with her was becoming too much to bear.

The beer was long finished before she left the bathroom. She came out, still wearing the sundress and stood in the living room without speaking for a minute.

"Are you all right?" Jerry finally asked.

"I made five hundred dollars."

"Well, that's good, I guess. But I could hear you in there. It sounded very painful."

"It was, kinda."

"Kinda?"

"Uh, well, it hurt when he was hitting me, but then he stopped and it felt... funny."

"Funny, good or funny bad?"

"Funny good, I guess."

"Come, sit down, let's talk more about it." He patted the seat next to him.

"Uh, no, thanks."

He suddenly got it. "Ohh... your bottom hurts, doesn't it?"

She nodded.

"Let me see."

"No! I'm too embarrassed!"

"Embarrassed? Because of me? Hell, I've seen you naked before, Jami."

She grimaced. "Why do you call me that? My name is Melissa."

"Sorry. I've just gotten used to it, I guess. It's better that I use that name then slip and use your real one around customers, isn't it?"

"Yeah, I guess you're right."

"I still want to see. I think you need a second opinion on how badly hurt you are."

"I'm not going to the doctor, if that's what you think!"

"No, no, I don't expect you would want to. But I think you should show me, just in case."

Jerry realized there was far more to his request than altruism. He wanted to see just what she had gotten herself into. Surprisingly, it made him hard.

Reluctantly, she turned away from him and lifted up her sundress. He whistled when her bright pink and red bottom came into view. "Wow, he really whipped you."

She craned her neck over her shoulder. "Yeah. Do you think it will be permanently marked?"

"Oh, no, those should fade pretty quickly, I should think." He paused. "So tell me, was it worth it?"

She dropped the hem before she turned around, afraid to show him her reddened pussy. "I'm not sure. I mean, five hundred bucks! And he said I could earn a lot more. He knows people who would pay it."

"Yeah, but at what price? You were with James one hour – what happens if you're with him all night? Or one of his sadistic friends?"

"That's the dilemma, isn't it?"

"I think it's far too risky, unless you've got some backup."

She nodded. "Yeah."

She hesitated and James could see something else was on her mind. "What? Is there something you're not telling me?"

Jami bit her lip. "Uh… he didn't use a condom."

Jerry stared. "Really? You let him?"

"Well, it was hard to stop him! He whipped me

and before I could recover, he was inside me! And he wouldn't stop."

"So you were raped."

She made a dismissive sound. "Yeah, call the cops. This whore was raped."

"I don't think of you as a whore. I mean…"

"I know you're just being nice. But that's what I am."

"So quit."

"I can't! I need the money."

"Come on, surely you've earned enough by now." He paused. "Which reminds me." He gave her an expectant look.

"Oh! Sorry." She reached into the pocket of her sundress and pulled out two hundred. "Do you have a fifty?"

"No. Give me a hundred and you can owe me."

She handed him the bill and said, "I'm good for it."

"I know you are." He wanted to get back to the topic at hand. "So how much have you earned, in total? How much do you have squirreled away?"

"Um… I'm not sure." She sounded evasive.

"Hey, I'm not going to rob you, if that's what you think."

"No, no! I didn't think that. I trust you, Jerry. You don't know how much."

"Yeah, thanks for that." *But you don't love me*, he thought.

"I guess, in the last few weeks, I've earned about eight grand."

"That's enough to put you up in a very nice place

for quite a while!"

"I know." She looked at the floor.

"So this is more about feeling comfortable. Protected."

She nodded. "Yeah."

"I can't continue to be a part of this. It would be different if you … uh, felt something toward me. But I'm starting to really worry about my job."

"I'll move out next week," she said softly.

"Look, I hate to do this. But you know how it is." Even as he said it, he knew he would miss her terribly when she finally left.

"I know you're right. It's just been nice, living here."

"And it was nice having you – up to a point."

"Has it really been that hard on you?"

Jerry decided to be honest. "Yes, yes it has. I hate to stand by and watch you turn into something… tawdry. I still think of you as that cute high school cheerleader, uncorrupted by life."

"Well, if life stood up for me for once, I might still be that girl!"

He stood and came over and gave her a hug. "I'm sorry. Your life has been hard. You didn't deserve any of it."

She cried against his chest. "You've been the only nice thing in my life. And I've been pushing you away!"

"Hey, now, you were right when you said I was too old. I know I am – you were just being honest with me. I can't fault you for that." He held her at arm's length so he could see her face. It was streaked with tears. "Look, I'm worried about you. I know you are making good money and all, but you need to get out of this business. If you do, you can continue to live here. If you don't, you have to move out. It's as simple as that."

"I know." She shook her head. "Part of me wants to go out and find a normal job – if I only could! – and the other part says, 'Get the money while you can!' Can you understand that?"

"I do. We all face temptation. I have been approached by kids for years, asking if I could get them some drugs. I could be making big bucks myself if I chose to go down that road. I also could have lost my job."

"So you think I should just take my money I've earned so far and go out and work at McDonald's for eight bucks an hour?"

Jerry pursed his lips. "I can't make that decision for you. You're an adult, you have to make it. I only told you what I had done in my life."

She nodded. "I get it. I have to think about it."

"I hope you can think on your feet, because your bottom appears to be too sore to sit down!" He said it as a joke to relieve the tension of the moment and it worked. She smiled and nodded.

"Yeah. He really enjoyed himself on my ass, didn't he?" She pulled herself free. "I'm going to go lay down for a while, okay?"

"Sure."

* * *

Melissa went into her room and closed the door. Jerry was right, but god! The money was so good.

After a life of not having anything that she didn't get from a thrift store, having to share every meal, having people look down on her as trash, she finally had some money!

She went into the closet and pulled out her beat-up suitcase and tossed it on her bed. She unzipped the compartment inside and pulled out the wads of money she had stashed, wrapped with rubber bands. Each wad represented a thousand dollars. She had seven of them, plus some loose bills. She took a fifty out she owed Jerry and added the four hundred and counted it again. In total, she had seven thousand, nine hundred seventy dollars. Nearly eight grand.

For reasons she couldn't explain, it didn't seem like enough. She tried to quantify her expenses. Let's see, eight hundred for rent, maybe another two hundred for utilities. Oh, she'd need a cell phone, that'd be another hundred. Food, maybe two-fifty? Clothing! Oh, she'd have to spend about five hundred a month on clothes for a while, if she was going to look the part of a high-classed call girl. That is, if she decided to go down that road. She still hadn't made up her mind.

In all, she could expect to face about sixteen hundred a month – and what about a car? She couldn't very well take the bus to her appointments. So it'd really be more like two thousand a month. Her cash would last four months. She would have to book more appointments just to keep up.

Now, what if I give it up, she asked herself. Take the eight grand and quit. I'd only need seven-fifty for a studio apartment, another one fifty for utilities.

Two-fifty for food. No clothing, no cell phone, no car. Just eleven-fifty a month to live like a pauper. If what Jerry says was true, I might only make eight hundred at some crappy minimum-wage job. My eight grand would last forever if I only had to dip into it for three hundred a month. *If I wanted to live like a pauper, working some minimum-wage job.*

The idea of going to work in some fast food joint, coming home every night exhausted, smelling like grease, didn't appeal to her. But she wasn't sure the life of a high-class whore was the right path either.

Maybe if she just got her own place, lived as cheaply as possible, but still dabbled in the business. She'd made so many great contacts! She could do it just for a little while longer. Until she felt more secure. So how much did she need before she felt comfortable? Ten thousand? Twenty?

The money was just too good to pass up, she realized. She gathered up all the money except for the fifty she owed Jerry and put it back in the suitcase. Monday, she'd go talk to the accountant. He could make some suggestions. Hell, she was already fucking him, why not pick his brain too?

Satisfied, she flopped down on the bed on her stomach and winced when her pussy hit the sheets. God, how that had made her feel! Her emotions were all mixed up. It was horrible and yet, she had come so hard she had nearly passed out. She felt all worn out after her session with James. It was odd, the effect he'd had on her. She'd been scared, sure, but it was arousing, she had to admit it. If she had just a few clients who paid her five hundred a pop for some kinky stuff, she'd easily make two grand a month. That's just four clients. Fewer if they wanted more hours with her. She could find a few men she could trust and she could handle it.

She'd never have to work in some crappy job, that's for sure.

Melissa dozed, thinking about the money, her bottom and pussy throbbing.

# Chapter Thirteen

"So, you want some professional advice, huh?" Norman Whitaker was in his office on Broad Street, dressed in a pale blue shirt and yellow tie, pulled loose. His suit coat was draped over the Aeron chair behind him.

It was a far cry from the last time she'd seen him, naked and grunting over her, his thick cock thrusting into her. He was about thirty pounds overweight and he had a pasty complexion of someone who stayed out of the sun. His thinning hair was combed straight back, making him look like a fat version of Nicholas Cage.

"I'm glad you came to me, Jami. I can show you some tricks of the trade. Or tricks of your tricks – ha!" He found himself amusing.

Melissa wasn't sure about him, but it seemed easier to have Norman help her than try to find some straight guy who would probably look down his nose at her current profession. She didn't want to have to explain herself.

"So, tell me what your goals are, huh?"

Melissa didn't know about something as lofty as goals. She was just trying to figure out how to afford her own place. "Uh, well, first, tell me what I should be doing with my money. It's all in cash, you know. I'm not sure I can just put that in the bank."

"No, no! Don't bank a big wad of cash. You have to be able to account for that. The IRS would be all over you and give you the Al Capone treatment."

"The what?"

"Al Capone. You know, the gangster in the twenties, who was killing people right and left, but the government could only get him on tax evasion. But it was enough. He died in prison."

"Oh. I don't want to wind up in prison."

"No, of course you don't. So we need a way to explain your income. Without telling them where it really came from, you dig?"

"How can we do that?"

"You need a laundry business. And that could mean literally. Buy a small Laundromat. Or a deli. Or an arcade. Anything where people routinely pay in cash. You mix in your earnings with the receipts and bingo, no one's the wiser."

"I can't afford to buy a Laundromat!"

Norman waved his hand. "You don't have to, by yourself. You can go in with someone, be a silent partner. I can ask around. There are always guys looking for investors."

"How do I know this investor won't try to rip me off?"

"If he did, you'd take your money out and find something else. The most you'd lose would be a month's earnings or something. And they guy would know that. He'd be an idiot to try and scam you."

"I'd rather run the business myself. Or with a partner I already knew and trusted." Suddenly, she thought of Jerry.

"That can be done. It will take a bit more up front, you see. But you can do it." He narrowed his eyes. "How much you got already, stashed away?"

"Uh, about eight grand."

"Wow, you're doing great! And some of that was my money!" He laughed again. "Speaking of which, I could use a quick BJ. You wanna earn an easy fifty?"

Melissa hesitated. She looked around. "Right here?"

"Sure. When I heard you were coming in, I gave my receptionist the rest of the day off. We're all alone."

"Okay, I guess. But wait – how much does it cost to buy a small business like that?"

"That can range from about sixty grand all the way up to two hundred thousand or more, depending on the size. But it's not just the business. You gotta have someone to work it for you, someone who knows what's really going on and can keep his or her mouth shut. So there are ongoing expenses, you see. I'd say, to really get in on the ground floor in a small shop, you'd have to expect to come up with ten-twenty grand to start and be making about five-ten grand a month."

"Th-That's a lot. Won't the business bring in some money too?"

"Oh, sure. But some do better than others. The best deals are the ones that are being sold because they ain't been doing too good on their own. You pick 'em up for sixty grand, add your earnings to it and suddenly, it's a booming business! You see?"

"Yeah, I guess I do."

"So you want me to start looking around for you?"

"Uh, I'm not ready to buy something for sixty grand! I only have eight."

"I know. But you've almost got the down payment. After that, you just gotta pay in installments. And from what I see, you're business is only going up, am I right?"

"I guess so. I've been looking for a regular job all summer and haven't found shit."

Norman made a dismissive wave of his hand. "A girl like you, workin' in some burger joint would be a crying shame. You got talent, girl. You've got class. I mean, look at you! If you got some nicer clothes, keep your hair done right, you could name your price. You could be earning ten grand a month easy."

"Really?" She was tempted. "Uh, I'm hoping to easy my way out of the business before too long. I don't see this as my career."

"Well, then you'd better find a business to buy that's not on its last legs, so it can survive after your influx of cash disappears. Personally, I think it's a shame, you giving up the biz. I for one would mourn."

Mel smiled. For all his bluster and bravado, Norman seemed a decent enough man. "And you can help me find something like that?"

"Oh, sure. You leave it to me." He pushed back away from the desk. "Now, about that BJ. I can't wait to feel that cute mouth on my cock."

Monday afternoon, Melissa was waiting for Jerry to come home. School had started and he was not expected until after five, which drove her to distraction. She had something important to ask him.

But first, to get him in a good mood, she was going to fuck his brains out.

She heard his car in the driveway and quickly stripped off all her clothes. She peeked through the blinds to make sure he was alone. He was. His head hung down as if he'd had a bad day. She would cheer him up!

He came in and did a double-take. His face lit up. "What's all this?"

"Tah-dah! Your surprise. Come on, you look like you could use a good fucking." She grabbed his hand and tugged him down the hall.

"Wait, I'm all sweaty!"

"I don't care. Come on!" She pushed him into her room and attacked him, peeling off his clothes. He did smell of sweat but she was used to his odor by now and wasn't offended. Within seconds, he was on top of her, thrusting hard and grunting.

He came and she pretended to as well. When he rolled over onto his back, she propped herself up on one elbow and looked at him. He opened his eyes and looked back.

"What?"

"I was thinking of something. Do you think you could manage a small business?"

"I've got a job."

"I know. This wouldn't interfere. You could do

this at nights or on weekends."

"What are you talking about?" He pushed himself up until he was propped up against the headboard.

"I need a manager."

"Oh, no, I'm not going to be arrested for managing some … prostitute!"

"No, not that. It'd be a Laundromat or a pinball arcade or something."

"What? I don't understand."

Mel explained Norman's logic and how the business would be legitimate to the IRS. "I just need someone in there I can trust. That would be you."

"Well, I'm flattered you trust me," he said. "So you'd pay me?"

"Of course! I don't know how much yet, but it would be in addition to whatever you get at the school. Think of it as retirement money or something."

"Sounds intriguing. But I'd have to think about it. I mean, it's still illegal. Now, instead of prostitution, you're talking about income tax evasion. I don't see how that's any better."

"But Norman says these things happen all the time and can go on for years without ever being detected. And when I retire, which will be soon, trust me, I can just run the business myself if I want. No more working for some other guy! I'd be my own boss."

"And what about me? You'd kick me out and take over?"

"We could work that out. I don't know. We're talking about a long time from now."

"Wait – you plan to be a whore for a long time?"

"I… I didn't mean it like that. I meant to say, I'd want you running my business for at least a year, maybe longer. That's a long time to me. And when I'm done, you can go back to being a janitor and not worry about being audited by the IRS."

"Huh. But how would it work, me running your business while keeping my job at school?"

"You'd have to hire someone to run the day-to-day operation. You'd come in to check on the books and the money."

"You mean cook the books."

"Norm can do all that. You just have to make sure my money gets mingled in and that the employees don't rip me off."

"Well, let me think about it."

"Please do."

"Uh…"

"What?" She saw something else just occurred to him.

"Could I still get… freebies?"

"Of course! You could fuck me anytime. I'd say it would be the cost of doing business."

His face broke into a big smile. "In that case, I'm in. I'll do it."

She hugged him. "Oh, that's great, Jerry. Thanks!"

\* \* \*

It wasn't until after dinner that the full impact of what Melissa had proposed sunk in. He'd still be involved in illegal activities, at least for a while longer, something he had hoped to give up. But balancing that out was his continued access to Jami, the whore. As much as he had wanted her out of his house, he hated to have to let her go completely. He could never get such a cute girl to fuck him otherwise.

And hadn't she said she'd only be doing this for another year or so, just until she could earn enough to pay off her debts and then she'd simply be another business owner. He could go back to his job, knowing that he had helped out a young girl – and gotten laid enough to last him a lifetime.

It sounded too good to be true. So why was he worried about it?

\* \* \*

Norman found Melissa a Laundromat for sale about four miles from Jerry's place. The owner wanted to retire and move to Sun City. It was small, with just a dozen washers and ten dryers. But the price was right – sixty-eight thousand. They were sitting in his car outside the place, watching the handful of customers do their laundry while they discussed the deal.

"I've checked his books and his tax forms. His income was legit – he's been clearing about two grand a month, after expenses. With your income, you could double that and no one would be the wiser," Norm told her.

For Melissa, it was happening too fast. She hadn't even decided if she wanted to continue working as a whore and now suddenly she was about to commit to a business? "How long do you think I'd have to do my, uh, sideline business, until this could pay for itself?"

"Probably never, but it's really just a front. I mean, this Laundromat never really made a lot of money –

that's why it's so cheap. You'd really need to expand and you've got existing businesses on both sides. But that's not really the point. You want to hide your earnings. You can leverage the business after a while to buy a bigger Laundromat and between the two, you might have enough to live on if you chose to retire. Which would be a crying shame, but, hey, I know where you're coming from."

"Right. You really think I can swing this by myself?"

"Truthfully, you'd probably need a partner on this. No bank is gonna think you got the collateral for it. And you can hardly tell them you make your living on your back!" He paused and snapped his fingers. "Wait a minute! If you're willing to fuck the guy for free, I think I know someone who might look the other way on the loan app."

Great, she thought, another freebie. "How often might I have to do this?"

"Oh, probably once or twice a month." He noted her reluctant expression. "Hey, it's all part of doing business. In this economy, sometimes you gotta make trades to get what you want. It's either this or, you get a partner."

"I'd rather be independent. Why don't you set up a meeting with this horny banker?"

"Great! I'll do that." He paused. "While we're talking, you know, we never really discussed my fee."

"Right. What do you charge for your part in this?"

"Well, I'm thinking of an ongoing relationship. You know, I do your taxes, keep you outta trouble with the IRS, bring you some customers… consider it a package deal."

Another Frank, she thought. Another guy she'd have to fuck for free to keep him happy. "So what do you expect from this package deal?"

He flashed her a Chesire cat grin. "Say six hundred a month, plus two fucks and two BJs a month."

Melissa shook her head. "Three hundred and one fuck and one BJ per month."

Norman sat back and tapped his fingers on the steering wheel. "Five hundred, one fuck and two BJs."

"Four hundred, one fuck and one BJ – but only until I retire."

"Girl, you drive a hard bargain." He waited a beat. "Okay." He stuck out his hand. "You've got a deal."

Melissa thought it was a pretty good one. She was proud of herself for negotiating. She shook his hand. "Shouldn't we have some sort of contract?"

Norm smiled. "You think it would be binding? No, it's better this way. If you can't trust your accountant, who can you trust?"

"I'm not sure I can trust anybody – except maybe Jerry."

"Oh, right, your boyfriend."

"He's not my boyfriend!"

"Oh, excuse me. You live with the guy and fuck alla time; I don't know what else you'd call him. Except maybe pimp."

"Yeah, I'm not sure what to call him either."

Within a week, Melissa found herself on her back in a very nice hotel room, fucking the banker. His name was Everett Sloan and he was actually quite handsome, with just a touch of gray in his hair. She noted he had on a wedding ring and wondered again why a man would want to cheat on his wife. Or was she just being naïve?

Sloan had made it clear he didn't want to wear a condom and she had protested, but it turned out to be a deal-breaker. Either she fucked him bareback or she wouldn't get the loan. So she gave in, but only after he convinced her he was clean.

"If my wife ever found out, I'd be in big trouble," he told her as he stripped off her clothes.

"All the more reason to wear a condom. You don't know where I've been!"

"A young girl like you? You look like you're still in high school. I'm sure you're very clean."

"I've been fucking guys for a couple months now and some of them don't wear condoms."

"Really? Well, I'll take my chances." With that, he pushed her onto the bed and climbed over her. He was still dressed and he simply unbuckled his pants and pulled out his stiff cock. Within seconds, he was inside her, thrusting hard. Melissa just lay back and pretended she was enjoying it.

It was such a simple act, really, she told herself. A couple of pumps, a squirt or two and it was over. In exchange, she got a lot. If she could only keep the shame from overwhelming her.

*I'll just do this for a year, then I'll retire*, she told herself again.

Sloan grunted and came and she felt his watery discharge soil her. She pretended to come as well and grasped him and told him what a great lover he was.

Now that he had come, he was all business.

"Okay, here's the deal, missy. I'll do the loan for fifty grand, no more. So you gotta come up with the rest. With closing costs and such, you're looking at maybe twenty grand." He held up his hand when she started to protest. "Now, now – Norm told me you got less than ten. But he also says you could earn another ten in a month if you work it right. So get busy. To stall, we'll put in an option on the place. That will cost you an extra thousand, but it will be worth it. You'll buy some time."

He got up and began zipping up. "Now, as to my end of the deal. I want a free fuck once a month until I say different."

"No, that's too open-ended," she responded. "I'll fuck you once a month for six months, no more. That's a deal-breaker. Otherwise, I walk away, go look for another banker with a hard-on. Think I could find someone?"

Sloan was clearly impressed by her bargaining skills. "Well, I didn't expect such sand from such a cute little girl. Okay, you got a deal. Six months. After that, if I want your services, I'll pay for them."

"Damn right."

They shook on in, Sloan fully dressed and Melissa naked. He laughed at the image. "If only I could conduct all my business deals like this!" He shook his head. "No, wait, that sounded gay or something. I meant with the women… No, wait, some of them I'd never want to see without clothes! Forget it."

They both laughed and Melissa felt better. She was getting good at this negotiating thing.

# Chapter Fourteen

From September fifteenth until October tenth, Melissa worked. She moved out of Jerry's house and rented a hotel room. She took on all the clients that came her way. She quickly established some ground rules, however. If a guy wanted to fuck her bareback, he had to bring a recent blood test and five hundred dollars. No exceptions. Otherwise, the price was two-fifty and she was getting it.

If one of James' friends called her for some spanking games, the price was five hundred an hour. If they wanted to fuck her without a condom, the price was seven-fifty and a clean blood test.

To enforce her new rules, Mel couldn't rely on Jerry. He was always at work – plus, he was just too nice a guy. She hired a bodyguard and went with the stereotypical bald, beefy black man, an English ex-boxer named Chauncy. He looked mean, but when he opened his mouth and that educated British accent rolled out, he sounded even more threatening – a thug with brains. No one fucked with Chauncy.

Jami, the whore, was soon rolling in dough. In the three weeks she concentrated on her business – and turned her mind off to the shame – she made another eight thousand dollars. It still wasn't quite enough to buy the Laundromat. With Norm and Sloan's help, she offered another thousand dollar option and gave herself another month. No one else had come forward to buy the small shop, so the owner was happy to make the deal.

She also bought a used car and with Jerry's help, learned to drive it. There were a few close calls before she remembered all the rules of the road, but she passed her driving test on the first try and was quite pleased with herself.

By November first, Jami had earned another nine thousand and had plenty of money to buy the business. She got the loan, paid the owner his down payment and took control of the Laundromat. She hired someone to handle day-to-day operations and named Jerry as manager. Truth was, however, that Norman handled the books and made sure the tax man was satisfied. Jerry was little more than a figurehead who came in now and then to check on the employees.

But Jami was happy to pay him to do very little. She felt she owed him.

The hardest part of her new life was the spanking games, although that's where the big money came. She was stunned by how easily the men parted with a thousand dollars or more just to be able to whip her with a riding crop, pussy whip, soft belt or cat o'nine tails. Jami had installed strict rules there too. No caning, no leather paddles – nothing that might cut her or bruise her too much and interfere with future clients. No man wanted to pay for a whore whose ass was all marked up.

She realized she could easily concentrate on the spanking aspect and make some really good money. There were many whores competing for the rich businessman trade, but not too many put up with the whippings.

Mel found her bookings began to reflect more BDSM and less straight fucking. That was okay with her – she wanted the big money up front. This was only temporary, she kept telling herself.

But she had to admit, she liked living the high life. The fancy hotel room, room service, the meals with clients at upscale restaurants. She was moving toward the "girlfriend experience" and she hadn't signed up with an escort service. She was doing it on her own, with the help of Chauncy, her accountant and Jerry.

It was a heady time for her.

And all she had to do was lay back spread her legs and smile. Oh, and pretend to enjoy it. She had learned the art of faking orgasms. Every client was made to feel he was special. Even the ones who wanted to whip her first – she learned to beg for mercy even though she could take the abuse. By controlling the instruments, she was able to handle the pain. And afterward, she could count on some big paydays.

Norman found her another Laundromat, a larger one, and she put a down payment on it at once. This one cost one hundred and fifty thousand but it cleared more than four thousand a month. It was easy now to spread her earnings between the two businesses and the IRS would have no clue what was really going on.

She still had to offer freebies to Norman, James,

Sloan and Frank, on occasion, but it was a small consideration. She actually looked forward to fucking Jerry, because he was so damned grateful. She found he was the only one truly in her corner and it made her realize just what a valuable friend he had been to her all these months. Without Jerry, she felt all alone in the word.

Everything went smoothly for the next few months. She made a lot of money and was already looking to buy a third business. Her world came crashing down one day in February. She had just agreed to fuck a new client, a man named Sean, who had come recommended by Everett Sloan. They had met in her hotel room and she had informed him of her prices when the door burst open and armed cops flooded into the room. Jami froze, thinking she was about to be shot.

Sean turned out to be an undercover cop.

She was handcuffed, arrested and charged with prostitution. She learned later Sloan's boss had discovered the shady loan and called him on it and Sloan gave her up. It was a simple matter for him to recommend the cop and she had fallen for it.

The hotel kicked her out at once and when she made bail, she had nowhere to turn but Jerry's house. Without an income, she couldn't afford another hotel and her savings went to support her businesses and pay her lawyer. It surprised her that Jerry welcomed her back and gave her the spare room without any questions.

"I'm sorry to hear about your troubles," was all he

said.

"My god, Jerry, how can you put up with me, after all this?"

He shrugged. "You're my friend."

It opened her eyes. Of all her clients, her business associates, only Jerry was in her corner through thick and thin. It made her feel terrible about how she had treated him so cavalierly.

"Jerry," she told him, putting her hand to his jaw. "You are my best friend, you know that?"

He dipped his head. "Oh, come on. You have lots of friends."

"No, I don't. I have acquaintances. I have clients. None of them stick around when the going gets tough."

He shrugged. "Well, for the record, I don't like what you're doing. Don't get me wrong – I understand why you're doing it. But I don't like it."

She smiled. "I know."

While she was out on bail, she rejected inquiries from all her customers, who, surprisingly, had continued to call despite the publicity. Melissa figured she could afford to live on her savings for a few months, as long as she wasn't convicted and sent to prison.

During her trial, her attorney made a big show about the "poor orphan girl who was tossed out on the streets because of California's failed safety net." When Melissa testified that she felt she had no choice but to turn to prostitution after more than three months of fruitless job searching, Jerry could see tears in the eyes of the women on the jury.

She was found not guilty.

The judge gave her a stern warning not to return to his courtroom and she was free.

She and Jerry celebrated with a quiet dinner at his house, followed by a very satisfying love-making session in his bed. She slept there and couldn't remember when she had felt so comfortable.

In the morning, she got up and tried to reorganize her life. Although the second Laundromat paid for itself, the first one was still a drag and needed to be subsidized. How could she do that without working?

She broached the problem with Jerry.

"So how long before you can make the first Laundromat a going concern?" he asked.

"I don't know. Maybe never. That was the attraction for it. I could toss in my earnings and it was doing fine. But if I don't work, how can I keep up the payments?"

"Doesn't the second Laundomat make enough to cover both?"

"Not yet. Maybe in a year or so."

"So what are you saying – you need to work for another year?"

"Yeah, although what if I get busted again? I doubt I'll get off this time."

"Hmm." Jerry looked at the ceiling. "It's a problem."

"Hey," she said, reaching out and cupping his hand into hers. "Do you think I'm a terrible person for what I've done? I can't imagine you're still putting up with me."

"Oh, no, I don't think that. I mean, sure it's not something I'd recommend, but I know how tough it is out there. I'm sure if the economy was better, you would have found more, uh, meaningful work."

She smiled. "You're the only guy I know who would remain so optimistic about my life."

He shrugged. "I told you, I couldn't have a Westmont girl living under a bridge."

"Oh, you've gone way beyond that. You've literally saved my life – many times."

"Hey, I've gotten a lot out of it. I mean, look at me. Not only have I made some bucks, but I've gotten my dream girl besides."

She dimpled. "I'm your dream girl?"

He backtracked. "Well, uh, I just meant from my point of view. I mean, I know how you feel."

She sat back and crossed her arms under her breasts. "Maybe I've made a mistake. And not because of the age thing – I think it's more about my immaturity."

He smiled. "Well, don't be hasty. Take your time. I'll be here."

That just made her appreciate him all the more.

"How could you say that after what I've done – all the men I've had?"

He shrugged. "I don't like it. I'm hoping you'll quit soon."

"I'm trying, Jerry, I'm trying."

Mel fired all the small clients and rejected anyone she didn't already know. That left a handful of James' friends, whom she accepted because she could make the most money. Stu, Frank and his friends were all turned away. Using the last of her savings, she paid off the bank loan promulgated by Sloan and when he called to apologize for turning her in, she claimed to not know what he was talking about, in case the call was being recorded. She asked him never to call her again.

She worked quietly for two more months until she had build up her nest egg once again. With Norm's help, she found an arcade that was available for a reasonable amount. Between the three businesses, she could make a go of it with just a few clients a month. She always went to a hotel room so as to not upset Jerry.

She had planned to give up the business entirely, but when she could make three or four thousand a month with just a handful of clients, she thought, Why not? And Jerry was surprisingly patient. She knew he didn't like it when she went out, but she paid him rent and she slept with him every night, so he was getting what he wanted. Sometimes, she had to wear a nightgown to cover the bruises on her bottom, pussy or breasts.

Out of the blue, Jerry asked her one night, "So, tell me, why do you continue to let men beat you?"

"Uh…"

"I'm serious. I'm not mad. I'm just trying to understand."

"It's mostly about the money. I can make a thousand or fifteen hundred a night and only work three-four nights a month. I know all the guys now and what they like. It's kind of like a ritual, you know?"

"I guess I don't."

"Well, they are very formal. They come in and

have this set protocol of what they want that's going to get them off. I'm sorry, but that's the way it is."

"I know. I have no illusions."

"So they select their instruments of… uh, stimulation and they apply them and I pretend it's horrible – that's a key thing I've found. They like to punish me, kind of like I'm a surrogate or maybe they just get off on it."

"Huh."

"But they never go too far – we have established boundaries by now. So they get it out of their systems and then they fuck me – I'm sorry, am I making you feel bad?"

"No, no. I'm fine."

He didn't seem fine to her, but she continued. "And afterwards, they go home happy and able to cope with their messed up lives a little longer. No one gets hurt. In many ways, I'm like a therapist."

"A sex therapist."

"Yes. Although I have no formal training. I just know what they need."

"Do they hurt you?"

"Sometimes they might go a bit too far. But I have safe words and they know if they ignore them, they don't get to come back. I've made that very clear. They need me, so they behave."

"Wow."

"I know. It's pretty kinky."

"You think you'll ever give it up?"

"Sure. After a while. I need to make my businesses go first."

"I don't feel I've been much help there. I mean, I

go to the businesses and check in, but you don't really need me. Norman handles the books. I just make sure the employees stay honest."

"Oh, you have no idea how much help you've been. Without you, I don't know where I'd be."

"I'm glad to do what I can."

She kissed him. "You are my hero."

"Oh, pshaw."

They made love and she came, a pleasing but not intense climax. What she didn't tell Jerry was that her orgasms were much stronger after her clients whipped her and fucked her. It was a huge turn-on and she often wondered why that was so. One of the mysteries of life.

"The Mexican restaurant next door to your Laundromat his going out of business. Do you want the space?" Norm asked her one day in April.

"What?" She was sitting in his office, the taste of his seed still on her tongue. The price of doing business with the accountant.

"It's an extra nine hundred square feet. You could double the size of the place. Put in some new services, too, like custom laundry and ironing. Or put in a bar if we can get the permits. I know the restaurant had a beer and wine permit. Having a beer while you do your laundry is a big attraction."

"Do you think I can afford it?"

"Sure. I mean, you'll need to subsidize the remodeling, but once it's up and running, this place should pay for itself. Remember, you've already paid off the loan, so it's just a matter of increased rent."

"Yeah."

"So with the three businesses, you should have a positive cash flow. You could retire. That's what you've been wanting, isn't it?"

"Yes." Now that it was possible, Melissa had to think. Did she really want to give up all of her clients? She had basically five – Norman, James and his friends Charlie, Dave and Randy. They all were married. Norman was a straight fuck or BJ. James and his friends enjoyed the spanking games they played.

And Mel had grown to like them too. In fact, she often wished Jerry wasn't such a nice guy. If he would whip her once in a while, he'd be perfect. How weird was that?

"Sounds good," she said quietly.

"Of course, I expect you'd want to keep a few clients, just to keep your hand in, right?" He winked at her. "I mean, I'd hate it if you gave me up."

"Uh, huh." She'd have to think about it.

"You need to give me an answer soon. Like tomorrow. The landlord would prefer an existing tenant took that place over, but he is considering other options."

"Do it," she said suddenly. "And try to keep the liquor license."

He nodded. "Now you're thinking like a business woman! I like that."

## Chapter Fifteen

"I can afford my own place, you know," Mel told Jerry one morning over breakfast. She was responding to his question about how much longer she would continue in her "sideline" as he called it. He considered her Laundromats and the arcade as real jobs. Decent jobs.

"I know. But didn't you say you wanted to quit?"

"I did." But that was before, she thought. She couldn't explain to a straight arrow like Jerry what she was getting out of it. Her attitude had changed. She thought back to the previous night, when James, one of her favorite clients, whipped her with the cat o'nine tails until she felt transported. It wasn't the first time she had "flown," as it was called in the vernacular, but it had been the most intense. When he had fucked her moment later, she had the single most powerful orgasm of her life. And then he paid her a thousand dollars.

How could she give that up?

She couldn't, but she didn't expect Jerry to understand. As much as she cared for the man, she realized he was not the right one for her. He had come close, but it just wasn't in him to be dominant. He was the stereotypical "nice guy" and would need to find a nice girl to settle down with and have kids.

Mel wasn't sure what she wanted in the future. Maybe she'd want to marry a decent man like Jerry and have children, when she was past thirty. For now, she wanted to continue what she was doing. Maybe buy another business or two. The transition from high-class whore to businesswoman would be so much easier then. But that was just what she would tell Jerry. The real reason was, she wanted to have more orgasms like the ones her clients gave her. After they spanked her bottom or breasts – or even her pussy. God, that was always so intense.

Dave was her favorite for those games. He was a short, heavyset man, not much to look at, but oh, god did he know how to handle a pussy whip! He knew just how hard to and how long to hit her with the small leather whip until she was begging him to stop. Of course, he ignored her, just as she wanted him to, because she never used her safe word with him. In the heat of the moment, she thought she would many times, but he would change the rhythm of his blows and she would begin to shake and she knew her orgasm was thundering toward her. He was the only one who could make her come just from the whipping. Afterward, their sex was almost anti-climatic.

And then there was Randy, the only one she let tie her up. He was a handsome man in his thirties, not unlike Jerry, but he was all dominant! Too bad he was married. His wife, apparently, did not like his little games. It had taken months for her to trust him. She made sure Chauncy was right outside, ready to burst in if she needed him. They had started off with light cords, just on one hand or foot, and worked their way up to a full hog-tying before he'd spank her. She used her safe word a lot with him at first. He always respected it. The feelings she got from being helpless made the sex so powerful, but in a different way than Jerry or Dave did. He usually whipped her until she used her safe word and then fucked her. God, she came two or three times in a row, like a string of firecrackers going off in her head.

How could she give all that up?

She couldn't, and she knew it. Which meant, it was time to leave Jerry's place. She had owed him, but after all the love-making they had done, it was time to end it. He wouldn't be happy. She had probably stayed too long as it was.

"Jerry," she said, putting her hand on his arm. "I really do need to move."

His face fell. "Really? You don't like it here?"

"It's not that. It's just time for me to have my own place. I feel I've overstayed my time here."

"But you're wanted. I mean, you can stay as long as you want. I was mostly against listening to you… you know."

"I know. The thing is, I know you don't approve of my lifestyle. For a while, I didn't approve of it myself, but I have come to realize, it's not all bad. Fucking guys like Stu and Frank made me feel cheap and dirty, but the clients I have now…"

"The ones who beat you?" He was incredulous.

"Yes, the ones who beat me. You make it sound awful. It's more like an art form, to them. And to me."

"Really?"

"Yes. I didn't think I'd ever be into something like that, when I started. James kinda opened my eyes."

"I don't like him."

"I know you don't. He's a dominant personality. Most lawyers are, I guess."

"Yeah." He looked away and Mel thought he might have tears in his eyes.

"I would never want to hurt you. You've been so good to me."

He turned back and said, "So continue to fuck me."

That caught her by surprise. "What?"

"Continue to fuck me. I'm not talking about every week or anything. Maybe just once in a while, you know?" He shook his head. "These past few months have been the happiest of my life. I was happy to help you and yes, I got a lot out of it too. And I try to understand your life now and I've come to accept it, even if I don't agree with it. But the thing is, I don't have a girlfriend and I like the closeness we've shared. So even if you move out, I know I'd miss you – a lot. Sex may be a poor substitute for a relationship, but it's all I'll have left."

She sat back. "You mean, like a freebie?"

He shook his head sadly. "You know I can't afford your prices."

Mel thought about it. He was a nice guy, what would it hurt? Maybe once a month or so, she could stop by and make him feel good. "Okay, but only until you find a girlfriend. And I want you out there looking."

He smiled and nodded. "Okay! That'd be great!" He hugged her.

She patted his back. "Okay, big boy, settle down. I've got to go out and start looking for an apartment."

"Want some help?"

"No, you've been enough help as it is. I can do this."

Melissa took a quick shower, grabbed her cell phone and hurried out. She called up a realtor she knew who specialized in all the right neighborhoods. She wanted something classy, upscale – and private. Mel could easily afford the top-of-the-line places and with the realtor's help, she quickly found what she was looking for in a small house tucked up behind a mansion in the hills with its own separate driveway. It was almost fifty yards from the main house, beyond the lawn and a large pool. The living room was generous and the bedroom and attached bath were luxurious. The kitchen was on the small side, but Mel didn't plan to cook much.

"It originally had been the maid's quarters, but it had been converted into a teenager's apartment," explained the realtor, a bleached blonde named Suzanne. "Now the teenager is grown up and gone and the homeowner wanted to rent it out – but only to the right tenant."

"Does he know about my… um… profession?" Mel had met Suzanne through one of her clients, so she was aware of what she did for a living.

"No, but I know the guy – he's a reprobate, so I know it wouldn't bother him. In fact, he might want to hire you himself."

She frowned. "I don't know. I'm not sure I want to mix business with tenancy."

"Don't tell him then. But if you started having clients here, he might find out."

"Yeah, I'll cross that bridge when I come to it." She looked around. "It's perfect. Are there others who want it?"

"Yes, but at this price, only a handful. I have a feeling you could get it if you flirted with the guy a little bit."

"Just as long as he knows I don't need a boyfriend."

"I'll make sure he does. Well, do you want to toss your hat into the ring?"

"Yes," she said. "It's perfect. Quiet, separate, and exclusive." The rent was a little higher than she had wanted to pay, but she could afford it.

"Great. Let's go up to the main house and I'll introduce you."

The man leered at her and said right away she was his top candidate if her finances checked out. His name was Anton Darby and Mel thought he sounded like a stuffed shirt. He was in his fifties, balding, intense and had a way of cocking his head as if he was trying to figure her out.

"So, what do you do for a living, if I may ask?"

Melissa had been prepared for this question. "Oh, my family has money and they helped me invest in some small businesses." She described her Laundromats and arcade.

He nodded. "Well, that's good. It's nice to see an entrepreneur at such a young age."

After a few more minutes of flirting with the old fart, he told her he'd let her know and she and Suzanne left. Outside, the realtor winked at her. "It's yours, I'm sure. The guy would love to have you around, I could tell."

"I just hope I don't have to fuck him."

"As long as you take your clients to a hotel, you should be okay."

Mel nodded. "Right."

Suzanne had been right. Melissa got the place and immediately paid the first and last month's rent and a security deposit before Darby could change his mind. Jerry was sorry to see her go.

"I'm trying to be realistic. I know we were never meant to be together. I mean, you're on your way to being rich and classy and I'm still a janitor."

"That's sweet, Jerry, but I'm just a whore. I'm not classy."

"Maybe not right now, if you want to look at it that way, but in a year or so, when your businesses are all self-supporting, you can give up this life and become a classy lady."

She smiled. "Yeah, maybe I will."

"So I can call you now and then?"

"Of course. And I'll come by and visit." They both knew what that meant. She stood on her tiptoes and kissed him. "Thanks. And I hope you find a nice girl someday. You deserve it."

"Thanks." He had that puppy-dog look in his eyes again and Melissa decided it was time to go.

"Well, I'm off. I'll call you after I get settled."

"Sure. Good luck."

She jumped into her car and started it up. She could really afford a better car, she thought. Something befitting her status as an independent business woman. Something else to put on the list.

\* \* \*

Jerry pushed his cart through the hallways, feeling depressed. He had been happy to help Melissa, but he missed her. She brought a light to his otherwise dreary existence. He knew he should be grateful that she would still come by now and then to fuck him, but it wasn't the same. He missed the company.

Maybe he was better off, he tried to tell himself. Look at Frank and Stu – they are supposedly happily married and they both sought Jami's services. If he found the "right girl" and married her, wouldn't he stray one day as well? Was it just in men to act like dogs?

He didn't have the answer to that. Nor did he understand why Jami seemed content to continue her lifestyle, letting men whip her and fuck her and do god knows what else! It baffled him.

"Jerry?"

He turned to see Amanda, a girl he only knew in passing. She was attractive in a bookish sort of way, with light brown hair and bangs. She was a bit of a loner, not very popular with the school's elite, and she didn't seem to care.

"Yes?"

"Uh, can I talk to you for a minute?" She tipped her head to indicate they move away from the other students.

"Sure." He wondered what this was about. They sat on a bench, his cart parked nearby.

"I live in the group home. You know, with Melissa before she left."

"Ohhh." His curiosity was piqued.

"Yeah. And now I'm in the same boat as her, only I don't have any cheerleader friends. In fact, I don't have any friends."

"Did she talk to you about me?" He was a bit worried about how much Melissa had told her.

"Yes. She said you saved her life. That you let her stay in your spare room until she got her feet under her and got a job. She said you were a really nice guy who didn't try to take advantage of her."

"You've talked to her? I mean, lately?" Jerry wondered if Amanda knew what Melissa was doing to earn money.

"No, not for several months. But she told me that if nothing else works out, maybe I could talk to you, you know, kind of like a last resort. Is that right?"

"Yes, that's right."

"So, what do you think? I mean, if Nancy can't find something for me?"

Jerry smiled. "So tell me, Amanda, when do you turn eighteen?"

Printed in Great Britain
by Amazon